I still remember my first sight of Barton Grove, towering above me. An imposing sandstone house, its Corinthian pillars framed a glossy black door. Some houses welcome you, but this one left me feeling unworthy of it, and all my old insecurities—a legacy from childhood—flooded back.

Joe caught me staring up at his home and laughed. "Come on, Chrissie, it won't bite you!" He fumbled in his pocket for his keys.

I smiled and shrugged, hoping the action would release the tension that threatened to spoil the moment. And I wanted nothing to spoil this moment. After all, this would be my new home. Mine and Joe's. With my head full of dreams and my heart lost to this man, I followed him up the short flight of steps.

Joe unlocked the door and, as he opened it, a chill breeze rushed past me from inside, and I caught my breath.

THE
SECOND
WIFE

CATHERINE
CAVENDISH

Dedication

To Colin, without whom…

Chapter One

Emily Marchant died on Valentine's Day. If only she'd stayed dead, how different my life would have been.

Of course, I can say that now, can't I? Now I know what she was capable of. As I sit here in my room, I can see everything so clearly. But hindsight gives us such wonderful vision, doesn't it? If I knew then what I know now, I would have run as far and as fast as I could and then run some more, to make sure I never heard the name Emily Marchant and never set foot in her house.

Because Barton Grove *was* her house and always would be. I was foolish to think otherwise. But I was young and so in love with my handsome doctor I would have crossed the Grand Canyon on a tightrope if he'd asked me to.

I'll never forget my first sight of him, as he sat at the bar in a central London hotel, staring into space. His fingers fiddled with a tumbler of Scotch and water. Such long sensitive fingers. Can a man have sexy fingers? If so, Joe's were.

I knew I was staring and that, at some point, he would become aware of it, but I couldn't tear my gaze away from that face, with its deep brown eyes and glossy black hair. I imagined how sensual it would feel to run my fingers through that hair. There were streaks of gray at his temples and every indication that he would age in Clooney-like perfection.

Despite nudges from my sister, Roni, accompanied by furious stage whispers to stop staring, I carried on. I sipped a gin and tonic and rolled an ice cube around in my mouth in what I hoped was a suitably seductive way. It might have worked for another woman, but not for me. I swallowed, it went down the wrong way and I was reduced to a fit of coughing that set my nose and eyes streaming.

That got his attention, although hardly in the way I would have chosen. He dashed over, uttered the timeless words, "Can I help? I'm a doctor," and began rubbing my back.

Ten months later we were married.

I still remember my first sight of Barton Grove, towering above me. An imposing sandstone house, its Corinthian pillars framed a glossy black door. Some houses welcome you, but this one left me feeling unworthy of it, and all my old insecurities—a legacy from childhood—flooded back.

Joe caught me staring up at his home and laughed. "Come on, Chrissie, it won't bite you!" He fumbled in his pocket for his keys.

I smiled and shrugged, hoping the action would release the tension that threatened to spoil the moment. And I wanted nothing to spoil this moment. After all, this would be my new home. Mine and Joe's. With my head full of dreams and my heart lost to this man, I followed him up the short flight of steps.

Joe unlocked the door and, as he opened it, a chill breeze rushed past me from inside, and I caught my breath.

"What's the matter?" he asked, taking my hand.

I was never a particularly fanciful person, never one to ask my mother to look under the bed for monsters when I was a child, or demand a night light; I had more than enough real horrors to worry about during my childhood. Now I was a sensible adult, and this was the man I wanted in my life forevermore. How could I tell him my heart was pounding for no reason? Or that a wind he had obviously not felt had nearly knocked me off my feet?

"Nothing," I said, pasting a smile on my face.

Joe took me past the oak staircase, along the dark hall and turned left through an open door that led into a spacious living room.

"Wow!" was all I could manage, as I tried to take it all in. A massive gilt-framed mirror hung over a traditional, white marble fireplace, where a full coal scuttle lay ready. Comfortable-looking sofas were positioned around the room. From the ceiling hung a huge chandelier, which would have looked ostentatious were it not for the magnificence of its surroundings.

Joe pressed the switch and flooded the room with light from bulbs that twinkled among the crystal pendants overhead. The room was painted a gorgeous pale lemon. Occasional tables were artfully positioned, and the walls were lined with imposing bookcases—the sort of bookcases in which a paperback would never have dared show its face.

This room had clearly been designed, rather than assembled by chance or circumstance. As for the designer, I was about to come face to face with her.

At some stage, a wall had been knocked down and two sizeable rooms had become one. Through a simple archway, the second half of the room was dominated by a framed photograph of a beautiful blonde woman, which hung above another marble fireplace. I was drawn to the photograph and moved closer, until I stood within a few feet. "Who is she?"

Joe sighed and ran his hand through his hair. "Emily. My late wife. I told you about her."

I nodded. I had only known Joe for a short time, but I felt as if I had known Emily for years. I knew her nickname had been Willow, and could see why. The face that stared back at me was undeniably beautiful, with high, aristocratic cheekbones and thick golden blonde hair that cascaded way below her shoulders. Her eyes were a vivid violet and her mouth, shaded a delicate pinky apricot, perfectly complemented her peaches-and-cream complexion. If the portrait had been full figure, I know I would have been looking at a slender, graceful woman with perfect poise.

Damn her! I thought to myself. I was keenly aware of what a contrast I must have been with my short dark hair, olive skin, and penchant for wearing jeans and T-shirts. After such perfection, what on earth did Joe see in me?

Maybe the photographer had used an airbrush, but I couldn't see one blemish on that beautiful face. The shot had been taken from an angle so that she wasn't quite full face. She was unsmiling. The set of her mouth and the way her eyes stared out at me gave her an enigmatic air. One hand was raised to her cheek, its long, perfectly manicured fingers clasping an exquisite cream-colored rose.

I stared long and hard at that photograph, taking in every detail, hardly aware of Joe telling me about the furniture and where Emily had found it all, who had decorated for them and the dinner parties she had hosted to raise money for all the worthy charities within a fifty-mile radius.

Perfect Emily. *Saint Emily*, I thought, as she gazed lifelessly down at me.

And then …

I stared, unblinking, sure I must have imagined it. Had that been a flicker of recognition? But this was a photograph. Emily was in her coffin six feet under Saint Matthew's churchyard. By now she was hardly more than a moldy skeleton. So why was I certain—if only for a fleeting second—that she had looked back at me?

"You're not cold are you?" Joe put his arm around my shoulder and we stood together in front of Emily's portrait.

"No, no I'm fine."

"But you're shivering. Shall I put the heating on?" His voice was uncertain, as well it might be. Outside, the sun shone on this unseasonably warm October day, and even in this large and airy room the temperature was comfortable.

Joe was waiting for an answer. I certainly couldn't tell him what I had imagined. "That photograph is so vivid, you'd swear she could climb out of it and join us here in the room."

"Yes," he said and I couldn't miss the tinge of remorse in his voice.

I tore myself away from her and took both his hands in mine. He smiled at me, head slightly on one side.

"You still miss her, don't you?" I said.

He sighed, lowered his eyes, and the smile faded. When he spoke, his words came haltingly, as if he were fighting back the tears. "I can't deny that these years without her have been hard. The hardest I've ever known. At her funeral, I wanted to throw myself into that grave with her. When they lowered her coffin and the priest did his 'dust to dust, ashes to ashes' bit, two of my friends had to hold me up. I've never known grief like it. Not even when I lost my parents." He paused and I wiped away a tear that trickled down his cheek. He took my hand and kissed it. "I thought I would never be happy again and I would devote myself to my work." He paused again. "But then I met you, Chrissie, and we had such an instant connection."

"But I'm so unlike her. She was so blonde and beautiful ... and look at me. No one would ever nickname me Willow."

He laughed lightly, clearly relieved to have told me of his grief.

From the day we met, our relationship had been intense. We always seemed in such a hurry to move things on to the next stage and, along with that, had come an urgent desire to learn about each other's innermost feelings and emotions.

I had never been one to talk much about myself. As a child, I learned early on to keep my mouth shut. "We don't tell others our private affairs," my mother said. I still remember her pale face and worried frown, as she admonished me for letting something slip to one of my school friends. My eight-year-old self never forgot those words. I did as I was told. Until I met Joe. With him, I could share those long-held secrets. I could be myself and open up as I had never dared to before. And he had told me about Emily, but, until that day, I had never seen him cry. I ached for him and also for myself. Would I ever inspire such love in him as Emily had?

Joe glanced up at the portrait and back at me. "I hated that nickname," he said. "She was always Emily to me. And don't do yourself down. You're gorgeous, and I wouldn't have you any different." He kissed the tip of my nose and that's when it happened. That's when I heard her voice for the first time. I flinched. Confusion filled his eyes.

I had to reassure him. "Sorry, I feel ... I don't know ... awkward, kissing you in front of her photograph. As if I'm stealing you away from her."

He clasped me to him and I leaned against his chest. He smelled of Hugo Boss aftershave, combined with his unique personal, clean aroma—warm, comforting, sensual. We stood there, wrapped in each other's silence. He gently stroked my hair. How could I tell him that I had heard a woman's voice whisper my name in my ear, as he kissed me?

The day after we were married, I moved into Barton Grove. Everywhere I went, I felt Emily's presence, her exquisite taste visible in every room. This house belonged in a glossy lifestyle magazine. I could picture the headline: "Mrs. Emily Marchant invites us to her exquisite Victorian home in idyllic Thornton Waterville." This would, of course, be superimposed on a full-page color photograph of her sitting on the edge of one of the sofas in her elegant living room. Her hair would be in a chignon. She would be dressed in a simple but stunning Chanel knee-length white dress, her slender legs perfectly poised in true finishing school style—together, but never crossed, angled to the left. Shoes? Chic, coffee-colored Jimmy Choos or Louboutin, none of their more flamboyant lines. Her makeup, immaculate as ever, would be simple, understated and her smile would be warm.

By the time I had imagined this scene twenty or more times, I had even decided that she would have simple diamond studs in her ears, a matching diamond on a gold chain around her neck and an expensive Gucci watch on her left wrist.

Her influence was also evident all over the kitchen. It had been furnished to resemble an idealized Victorian country farmhouse, complete with traditional oak cabinets, a Welsh dresser, and an Aga range. It also boasted a central oak table and six chairs. That kitchen could have comfortably accommodated a dinner party, but Joe couldn't remember the last time all the chairs had been used, except for some village committee meetings.

"There were usually just the two of us. Neither Emily nor I had any family to speak of and, of course, we never had children. But that's how she wanted it, so …"

And that pretty much said it all. Their marriage had been driven by what Emily wanted. And what Emily wanted, she invariably got.

Six weeks into our marriage, I began to feel increasingly restless. I had moved sixty miles to live with Joe and had given up my job as a university librarian. "You don't need to work," Joe said. "I can look after us both. Heaven knows I earn enough."

After twelve years of increasing job cuts and with more and more work being piled onto fewer and fewer staff, the prospect of being able to organize my own days and do what I wanted with my time was appealing, so I opted for "voluntary disengagement" — the university's euphemism for voluntary redundancy — apologized to my disgruntled fellow workers, and left without looking back.

For the first time, I wondered whether I had done the right thing. Here I didn't even have the housework to occupy me. Joe's cleaner had agreed to stay on. Mary came in twice a week, said very little, worked hard, and left. She did a great job and seemed to really enjoy it. How could I sack her? Besides, housework and I had always enjoyed something of an ambivalent relationship.

But when I realized I had rearranged the ornaments three times in as many days, I knew I must do something. So, on a sunny morning in August, as I sat in the rose garden on one of Emily's Victorian-style garden chairs, I thought through my options. I decided I needed a project to focus on. I also needed to take possession of this house away from Joe's deceased first wife. In short, I needed to redecorate. At last, I had made a decision!

"Yes!" I punched the air and two startled sparrows took to wing.

I took my coffee cup back to Emily's kitchen and almost skipped into the study, where I booted up my laptop.

The study was my favorite room, as it seemed largely untouched by Emily's hand. Joe had told me she had left it pretty much up to him, once she had chosen the wallpaper and curtains. For once she had compromised on her preferred dark velvets and had chosen blue brocade with a pattern of classical flower urns woven in golden thread. The window looked out of the side of the house at shrubs and a hedge. Nothing too distracting, so that Joe could concentrate when he was doing his medical research or writing up notes.

"It's a constant battle to keep up to date these days," he told me. "There are so many advances. Can't afford to get left behind." He would disappear into the study for hours on end. And that on top of a long day with surgery and visiting patients too sick to come to him.

It's no wonder I felt lonely. Hopefully my new project would absorb me. I only hoped I could create something as spectacular as Emily had.

That night, I couldn't wait for Joe to come home. I prepared his favorite dish—rump steak, with a creamy pepper sauce, flavored with cognac—and was waiting for him with a glass of champagne when he arrived.

He set down his medical bag in the hall as always and smiled at the sight of the chilled glass. "You read my mind," he said, taking it from me and brushing my lips with his. "It's been a scorcher today. I thought I was going to melt in that surgery. Even with the blinds drawn, the sun pours in. I know it's an awful thing to say, but I'll almost be glad when summer's over. Maybe then I'll be able to breathe again."

He took a deep swig, half draining the glass, and exhaled noisily.

I laughed. "There's more in the kitchen, sitting in a bucket of ice."

He rolled his eyes in ecstasy. "Lead me to it."

He took my hand and followed me down the hall into the shady kitchen. Overhead, the ceiling fan whirred. Its breeze ruffled my hair and cooled the thin film of sweat on my forehead.

"Something smells good," he said, wrinkling his nose appreciatively.

"Your steak's all seasoned and ready for firing, so it'll be nice and rare, just as you like it. I've only got to add the cream to the pepper sauce and we're all done. I've prepared a green salad as it's so hot today and there's garlic bread keeping warm in the oven. That's probably what you can smell."

"And I bet your steak's keeping the garlic bread company." He pulled a disapproving face. "I don't know how you can bear to eat the cremations you seem to enjoy so much."

I laughed. "Just because you like your meat still galloping around the field doesn't mean we all have to. Let's celebrate our differences."

Joe waved an imaginary flag in the air. "*Vive la difference!*"

We both collapsed into giggles. He set his glass down on the table and grabbed me around the waist, before kissing me long and deep.

"Mm," he said, as our lips parted. "I do love coming home to you, Mrs. Marchant."

"And I love it when you come home to me, Mr. Marchant. And you're going to love the idea I have."

"You'd better tell me all about it over dinner."

"I fully intend to," I said and poured more champagne.

If only I had stopped right there. If only I hadn't insisted on telling him my grand ideas for the house.

"If only …" The saddest words in the English language.

Chapter Two

Joe shoved his plate away from him, and stood up. "Why the *hell* would you want to rip out perfectly good furniture? What's the *matter* with you?" He kicked the chair back, marched over to the window and ran his fingers through his hair, his hands trembling.

I sat there in shock, my fork poised half way to my mouth. I had never seen Joe like this. When he looked at me, his face was red with anger.

I lowered my fork onto my plate and struggled to keep my voice calm. I knew I mustn't let my emotions overtake me, or this would end in our first row. "I want to put something of me into this house, Joe. It's only natural. At the moment I feel like I'm living in Emily's home—"

"Well you are," he said. "She spent months and thousands of pounds doing this house up, turning it into a home anyone would be proud to live in. Anyone, it seems, except *you*."

I fought hard to maintain my composure, but my emotions were too strong. "I can't believe you're being so pigheaded about this. Can't you understand? It's like living with a ghost."

"Don't be so melodramatic. Look, if you're so bored, why don't you do what Emily did? *She* was never bored. *She* was always busy with her charity work."

"I'm not Emily."

"No. You're not." He strode out of the kitchen, banging the door behind him.

I stared at the forlorn, half-eaten steak. Its blood stained the garlic bread at the side of his plate. A large tear meandered down my cheek and splashed onto the table, followed by another and another, until the dam burst and I sobbed my heart out.

Five minutes later, I heard the front door slam. Joe had gone out, leaving me alone once more.

I told myself to snap out of it. I dried my eyes, blew my nose, heaved a deep sigh and gathered up the debris of our half-eaten dinner. I necked the remains of the rapidly warming champagne from the bottle, which sloshed in six inches of melted ice, and threw it in the recycling bin, where it smashed against a small collection of wine bottles. For once, I remembered to scrape the food off the plates into the compost bin. Before my marriage, I had lived on the sixth floor of an apartment block. My kitchen had been so tiny, I could barely fit in one all-purpose waste bin, let alone the four I now had — each one color-coded to indicate permitted contents. Ignoring the dishwasher, I washed the dishes by hand, as I stared out of the window onto the terrace, which ran along the back of the house.

Suddenly, I felt hot breath on my neck. Thinking that Joe must be back, I spun round — no one there. Could I have imagined it? I stood for a few seconds, my heart pounding. Nothing stirred.

"Joe?" I called. But no one answered. I *must* have imagined it. I shook myself and wished the hairs on the back of my neck would settle down.

You're too tense, I told myself. *You need to relax, unwind.*

A long soak in a deep bath usually produced the desired result, so I ran the water and added my favorite bath oil.

I leaned back, closed my eyes, and luxuriated in the warm, fragrant water. *Mustn't fall asleep*, I told myself. But I found myself drifting, as my muscles relaxed and the tension in the back of my neck dissolved.

The house was almost silent. The only sound was the slight lapping of the water as I shifted position.

The scent of jasmine floated into my nostrils from the bath oil. Warm, sensuous. I drifted further, poised in that neverland between wakefulness and slumber.

And that's when the smell of vanilla poured over me. Something pulled me down in the bath. My eyes shot open and I struggled to sit up, a second too late. I tried to scream, but water poured into my mouth. I thrashed out, desperate to find purchase. Something was weighing me down. Something I couldn't see or hear. Blackness descended. I was drowning.

From somewhere, a new strength took hold of me, and with a huge push I emerged, coughing and spluttering, bathwater and saliva pouring from my nose and mouth as I took hold of the sides of the bath and hoisted myself out.

I stood on the sodden bathmat, bent double, retching and trying to catch my breath. I reached for the towel and buried my face in its reassuring softness. By the time the coughing subsided, my throat was raw, the lining of my nose burned, and my eyes stung. I was shaking all over.

Wrapped in the towel, I sat on the toilet and dried my face. My teeth started to chatter, even though I was warm. I looked at the bath. Water had splashed everywhere, splattering the wall tiles, turning the floor into a puddly mess. I shivered.

I had fallen asleep, I reasoned. That had been why I felt as if something was pulling me under. My brain had gone to sleep, so my muscles had ceased to function properly. It sounded plausible enough, and there couldn't be any other explanation, could there?

If only I had understood why I had smelled vanilla so strongly.

Joe came home at ten thirty. I heard the door slam and held my breath. I prayed he wouldn't continue our earlier fight. I was still unnerved by my experience in the bath and hadn't any energy for another argument.

My muscles tensed as I hugged my knees under my chin, on the sofa, oblivious to the drama unfolding on TV and far more concerned with the one unfolding in my own life.

The door opened and I glanced round at him. I ached to ask him where he had been, but knew the best idea was to wait and see what sort of mood he had returned in.

I soon found out. He hurried to the sofa, took my hands and raised me up. I could smell the whisky on his breath before he kissed me. Judging by the slight sway in his gait and his slurred speech, he hadn't stopped at one drink either.

"I'm sorry, Chrissie. I shouldn't have sounded off at you like that. Especially after you went to so much trouble over dinner and the champagne. That was a lovely gesture and deserved more appreciation. Am I forgiven?"

Emotion was closing my throat. I couldn't speak, so I merely nodded.

Joe continued. "I went to the Golden Compass, bumped into Martin Glendower. We were at university together. You remember? He came to our wedding, with that odd woman?"

An image flashed into my mind of a tall, blond guy around Joe's age with a flashing smile and permatan. His companion had indeed seemed a bit strange. She was all floaty chiffon, auburn ringlets cascading from a top knot, and heavy, kohl-rimmed eyes that made her look like a panda.

"They're not together anymore, by the way. Martin said he couldn't stand the constant smell of patchouli and the need to chant four times a day."

I found my voice at last. "I thought that sort of thing went out with Woodstock."

Joe went over to the drinks cabinet, opened it, picked up a bottle of Teacher's Scotch, paused, and replaced it before closing the cabinet again.

"Better not," he said. He smiled and raised his eyes. "My patients might not appreciate the fumes tomorrow."

Now he was in a better mood, I longed to broach the subject of redecoration again, but a little voice inside me counseled against it and I decided to wait. "Better the day, better the deed," as my late mother used to say.

The next morning, Joe took a couple of ibuprofen with his morning coffee, managed three bites of toast and downed nearly a pint of fresh orange juice before he gave me a peck on the cheek and grabbed his bag and jacket.

"See you this evening," he called, and was gone, leaving me with my thoughts as another empty day stretched in front of me.

The old railway station clock steadily ticked away the seconds and minutes, its rich tone comforting and soothing as I sat in the kitchen, contemplating nothing in particular. With little better to do, my mind meandered down all sorts of lanes, and if anyone had asked me my thoughts right then I would have been hard-pressed to tell them.

Finally, my coffee cup drained, I put my hands on the table, stood up, and made my way out into the hall. Enough daydreaming. Today I would do something constructive. Maybe Joe wouldn't let me redecorate, but at least I could tweak here and there. Anything to make the place more mine and less *hers*.

I made my way into the living room, determined to rearrange it in some way and I knew exactly where I would start. I marched up to the fireplace and stared up at her photograph with what I hoped was a suitably defiant gaze. For some reason, I was attracted by the rose in her hand. I noticed a detail I had missed before. A thorn. A small one, but one that was easily sharp enough to draw blood if you pricked yourself on it. For some reason, the thought unnerved me. A memory of last night's incident in the bath flashed through my mind and I knew my heart was beating faster. I didn't want to look at Emily anymore.

My gaze drifted down to the mantelpiece below her portrait. Six Lladro figurines adorned its surface. I wrinkled my nose. I didn't care how valuable they were, I hated them. Well, today was the day I would do something about them. I took deep, calming breaths and, carefully, I took them, one by one, over to a display cabinet which currently housed another of Emily's collections. I decided the porcelain ballerinas would fit right in among the Dartington crystal.

I had hoped to make myself feel better by my actions, but I still felt agitated and on edge—feelings that seemed heightened by my proximity to that portrait. I had a strong urge to get out of that room but I was equally determined to achieve something today.

I had an idea. The attic! It ran the whole length of the house. This was where, according to Joe, Emily had put the stuff she no longer wanted or couldn't find a home for. Maybe I would learn more about her up there.

As I made my way up the two flights of stairs, my mind drifted back to our wedding. On that gloriously sunny, late June day, I was introduced to the great and the good of Thornton Waterville society. Of course they had all known Emily and were at great pains to express their admiration for her.

The Chairwoman of the local Children's Society was especially effusive. "She was such a clever fundraiser," Mrs. Hope-Collins said, "and her cupcakes raised hundreds every year at the Summer Fair. Do you bake, Chrissie?"

"No, I'm sorry, I don't," I replied.

Her face morphed from curious to disappointed. "Oh well," she said, as her eyes focused on a spot some way over my left shoulder. "Never mind, I'm sure you have … other talents." She moved on, rapidly followed by Mrs. Neville, Miss Grace and Major and Mrs. Fernyhough, all of whom seemed less than impressed with the new Mrs. Marchant.

Only one was kind enough to linger. Diane Sterling was about my age, and taught at the local primary school. "Don't let them get to you," she said, squeezing my arm. "They're a bunch of old gossiping biddies who like nothing better than to ruin reputations over tea and crumpets." She gave me a knowing wink.

"You too?" I asked, relieved to find someone I could actually talk to.

"I'm an incomer like you. I came from London seven years ago, so they don't trust me here yet. You have to live here for at least a generation before anyone really accepts you. Unless you're the local GP of course, or the vicar. Your predecessor was all right because she was born in the next village, so she achieved honorary residency status. I have also committed the heinous sin of being able to neither bake nor sew — and as for crocheting …" She rolled her eyes.

I liked Diane. As I reached the top step and crossed over onto the landing, I decided to call and invite her over for coffee. The school holidays were over, but there was always Saturday morning. Most weekends, Joe was tied up with work in the study, leaving me scratching around for something to do.

Today was my first foray onto the top floor. I had simply not had any reason to go there before. A different world greeted me. These would have been the servants' quarters when the house was first built. I looked around and systematically opened one door after another, revealing a cornucopia of treasures, mixed in with the detritus of generations of this house's inhabitants. In one room, an old wind-up gramophone, perched on a small wicker table. On the floor beside it, a pile of dusty 78s lay, scattered. I bent down and picked up a handful, surprised at how heavy they were. Each was in its own sleeve. Artists my grandmother had liked—Bing Crosby, Jack Teagarden, Glenn Miller. I wondered if the gramophone still worked and resolved to try it out one day. But not today. Today, was a day of discovery. Carefully, I placed the records back on the floor and wandered off into the next room.

This revealed two single beds with rusting frames and thin, stained mattresses. Servants' beds no doubt, but here too, other, more valuable items had been deposited. Six old-fashioned, mahogany dining chairs were stacked against one wall, while, against another, stood a Singer treadle sewing machine and an empty Art Deco walnut display cabinet.

Two more rooms revealed yet more decaying beds, along with cracked ewers, broken furniture, discarded photographs, and even plates from a Royal Albert dinner service.

I turned the handle of another door and it opened reluctantly. Sun flooded through small, grimy windows illuminating an old, rusting cot, broken toys and discarded, moth-eaten rugs. Clearly this had once been the nursery.

The last door opened onto a very different scene. At the far end, stood a cheval mirror and next to it, a fairly modern orthopedic chair, the sort that is electrically powered so that the sitter can raise the base to put their legs up, lower the headrest and raise and angle the seat to enable them to sit and stand without discomfort. In short, the sort of chair designed for someone infirm and unable to cope with the kind of sofas Emily had installed downstairs.

In contrast to the other rooms, this room was relatively tidy. Some boxes of paperbacks lay scattered on the floor, no doubt ousted from Emily's smart bookcases. But for some reason the chair intrigued me. Who had it belonged to? I made my way across the dusty red carpet until I reached it. I stroked the chenille fabric and examined my hand. No sign of dust here.

I tested the seat with my hands and it seemed well sprung. No protesting groans or immediate signs of broken springs. Gingerly, I lowered myself into it, finding it firm, but comfortable. I settled back and reached for the control, which was stuffed into a specially constructed side pocket. I pressed one of the buttons. Nothing. I looked down. Of course, it wasn't plugged in. I looked around, but I didn't see a socket, so clearly this chair had been somewhere else before it had ended up discarded here. It was a shame, because those chairs were expensive. It would have taken some effort to get it up here too. With all the mechanisms inside it, this chair was heavy and cumbersome.

I shifted around, placed my hands on the arms and leaned back. As I did so, I caught sight of my reflection in the mirror. I certainly looked comfortable. I smiled and my reflection smiled back, but became lost in a black haze that descended in front of my eyes.

I panicked. I couldn't move. I tried to sit up, but something held me down in that chair. I couldn't scream, or even make the slightest whimper. When I willed my hands to move, something gripped my arms.

The sun had disappeared and the room grew darker and darker. From all four corners, shadows crept in, like a shroud descending on the room. I was certain someone was watching me. Someone else was with me in that room.

My heart pounded in my ears and a sound like rushing wind filled my head. I managed to open my mouth, but still no sound would come. As suddenly as it had descended, the haze lifted and the sun returned.

My reflection stared back at me with a deathly pale face and wide eyes. My hands gripped the arms of the chair and I had to will my fingers to let go.

I had imagined it, I told myself. Nothing had held me there. Only my own crazy fear had disorientated me. There had been a dark cloud, or maybe a partial eclipse of the sun. That's why it had grown suddenly dark.

I knew if I told myself this, I would calm down. So I kept telling myself and I did calm down. But my self-delusion was shattered when a voice spoke, close to my ear. "He will never be yours and this house will never be yours."

I stared at my reflection and screamed when I saw I was not alone.

She only lingered for an instant before she melted away. But she had stayed long enough to achieve her purpose. Tall, with wispy white hair that hung in listless strands around her deathly pale face, the wraith's eyes were like black pools, her head skull-like, almost fleshless. I was aware of some white fabric clothing her, but had no time to make out its shape before she was gone.

Alone once more and still rooted to the chair, I broke out in a cold sweat. I struggled to stand but the chair seemed somehow to draw me into itself. The angle changed. I tilted forward and heard a sound of a whirring motor. The chair moved.

I caught a glimpse of the plug, lying on its side on the floor. It should not have been moving. Nothing was powering it. I twisted from side to side in vain, but it had me in its grip and would not let me go. I screamed again, knowing that no one could hear me.

The motor stopped. I was at such a steep angle that I should have fallen, but still it held me until… Without warning, I pitched forward and had to grab the cheval mirror to steady myself.

I sobbed, with a mix of relief and fear, glanced back at the raised and tilted chair and dashed to the door.

It slammed shut before I reached it.

"Let me out!" I yelled and tugged at the ancient door handle, twisting and turning it, but it wouldn't budge. Behind me, I heard footsteps coming closer. I gritted my teeth and, still hanging onto the door handle, slowly turned around. A chill breeze brushed past my face, ruffling my hair.

Out of the corner of my eye, I sensed a rapid movement, like someone scurrying across the far end of the room. But I could see nothing there. Nothing unusual, except a strong scent of vanilla. At last the handle turned. I tugged it and the door opened easily.

In a flash, I was out of the door and I slammed it behind me, noting that there was no key on either side of it. It couldn't have jammed; it had opened too smoothly for that. Someone had locked me in there and, much as I hated to admit it, I was convinced that whoever—whatever—had done this, did not belong in my world.

Down in the living room, I poured myself a cognac. It was only eleven in the morning, but I needed it. My hands shook so much that I nearly dropped the bottle. It clanked against the crystal brandy balloon as I concentrated on setting it back down in one piece.

I took a deep swig and the strong liquor warmed and relaxed me. I wandered over to Emily's portrait and stared up at the lovely face. "Was that you?"

I stared at the portrait as I sipped my cognac, memorizing every inch of those perfect features and thinking, not for the first time, that there was far more to this woman than met the eye. Nobody could be as perfect as Emily. Again, I was drawn to the rose. A perfect rose, marred by a thorn. My imagination must be playing tricks on me because it looked even more vicious.

A cold shudder overwhelmed me and I hurried out of the living room, into the kitchen. "Get a grip, girl," I told myself.

On an impulse, I called Diane Sterling, glad she had given me her number at the wedding. She answered her cell almost immediately.

"Oh, hi Chrissie, you caught me on a break. Yes, I'd love to come over for coffee on Saturday."

"That's great. I wanted to pick your brains actually."

"You'll have to find them first. What about?"

"How well did you know Emily?"

"Not very. Didn't really have anything much in common with her. I always thought she was a bit … well … superior, if you know what I mean. I felt she looked down on me."

"So you knew Joe more than her?"

"Yes, but again, not very well. I was a bit surprised to be invited to your wedding actually, but Joe said he wanted you to have someone more your own age to talk to. He was a bit duty bound to invite the old biddies, because Thornton Waterville's that sort of place. It's a disadvantage of being a quaint village. Attitudes can be stuck in a time warp. A Victorian one at that." She laughed.

I couldn't even manage a smile. "I would really appreciate a chat, anyway. Something happened this morning and it's completely unnerved me."

"You do sound flustered. What happened?"

The words spilled out, unchecked. "I was in the attic and thought I heard and saw something. Then I seemed to be trapped in there and couldn't get out. There was this orthopedic chair and ..."

"Good grief!" I heard the distant sound of a school bell. "Damn! I'll have to get back to my little horrors. Are you going to be all right?"

I took a deep, calming breath. "Yes, I'll be fine. Honestly." I didn't tell her that the main reason for my assurance was a triple Remy Martin.

My head still searched for rational explanations. Had I fallen asleep and had a nightmare? Had a window been open, caused a breeze and allowed voices from outside to waft upwards and inside? Had my eyes been playing tricks on me? Did the chair have some sort of back-up battery which had kicked in? Had I turned the door handle the wrong way? Each of these explanations seemed hopelessly contrived, but I played and replayed the scene in my mind, until I was ready to accept that maybe, just maybe, my mind had played tricks on me and I had imagined it. It didn't sit comfortably with me, but the alternative was accepting that it had really happened, and that seemed far worse.

After a light lunch of a cheese sandwich, I forced myself back into the living room and searched Emily's bookcases for an absorbing novel, but shelf after shelf revealed leather-bound classics that looked as if they had never been read. I located *Wuthering Heights* and opened the green cover. The unique scent of a new book greeted my nostrils. No way had she read this one. The books were all for show, I decided. The ones she actually read were lying in boxes in that dreaded room in the attic.

I hadn't read Emily Bronte's classic for years and it seemed just right to take my mind off my frightening morning. Curled up on the sofa, I started the dark tale of doomed love on the Yorkshire moors.

My phone rang, I picked it up and saw 'Private Number'. I was tempted to ignore it as I usually did with such calls, but this time I answered it. "Hallo?"

Silence.

"Who is this?"

Silence. The line went dead.

Five minutes later it rang again, with the same result. Then again, and again. The sixth time it happened, I had really had enough. I switched the phone off and the calls stopped.

My concentration broken, I decided on a long, cold glass of mango juice and made my way to the kitchen. I had just opened the fridge when I heard the crash. It had come from the living room. I dashed in there and stopped dead. On the floor, resting against the wall and staring over at me, was Emily's portrait. Miraculously, the glass hadn't broken and neither had the heavy gilt frame. I stood frozen for a minute before daring to make my way over to it. Once there, I screwed my eyes up and peered up at the hole where the photograph hook used to be. I looked down and located it on the floor a foot or so away from the photograph. I bent to pick it up, thinking to place it on the table for Joe to re-hang when he got home. I had a thought. Why should he hang it up again? I was his wife now. Why should I have to stare at his first wife's face every time I walked into her room?

"Oh for God's sake," I said out loud, "I'm doing it again. It's *not* Emily's living room. It's *mine*. Mine and Joe's." I picked up the photograph and held it at arm's length. "Look, I'm sorry you died, Emily. I'm sure you were a very nice person and kind to small, furry animals. But the truth is, you did die. Joe loved you very much and took five years before he found someone else. Because he has doesn't mean he loved you any less. It just means he has his life to live. And he's chosen to live the rest of it with me." I was so glad no one could see or hear me.

But the violet eyes gazed out at me and, again, I had an uncomfortable feeling that they really were seeing me. The ends of my fingers began to tingle—a weird sensation like pins and needles. I decided to leave the photograph where it had fallen and propped it up against the wall. Joe could decide what he wanted to do, but I would at least try and persuade him to store it somewhere else. Perhaps in that attic room, along with her mirror and that chair.

Yes, the chair. It bothered me more than anything. I decided I really must ask him about that. But something else bothered me and my eyes darted to the mantelpiece. I couldn't believe what I was seeing. I edged closer, but there was no mistaking it. There, equally spaced along the surface, were Emily's Lladro ballerinas. I spun round to face the display cabinet. The door was closed. The Dartington crystal twinkled and the scent of vanilla wafted over to me.

Just after six, I heard the key turn in the front door and ran out of the kitchen to meet Joe in the hall. He smiled at me and landed a big kiss on my lips.

"What have you been up to today?" he asked as we strolled, arm in arm down the hall and into the living room.

He saw the photograph. "How on earth did that happen? Or did you take it down?"

"No, it managed to get there all by itself. I wondered if it was trying to tell us something."

"Like what?" Joe's voice had a suspicious edge to it, as if he still wasn't sure I hadn't sabotaged the portrait.

With a struggle, I kept my voice light. "Oh, that maybe Emily's ready to move on and have her photograph stored away somewhere."

His dark eyes flashed anger, which seemed to have erupted from nowhere. "Here we go again. Wanting to change things. You knew I was married to Emily for eight years. You knew she died tragically young. I can't forget all about her and sweep her away as if she never existed."

"Joe," I put a hand on his arm and he shrugged it off. But I was determined to have my say this time. "I'm sorry, but try and see it from my perspective. How would you like it if *I* had been the one to be married before? If *I* insisted that a massive portrait of my late husband dominated our living room?"

Joe stared at me, his lips tight, but at least he seemed to be thinking about what I had said. Eventually he spoke. "OK, Chrissie, I understand what you're saying, but this photograph is a work of art in itself. Can't you see that?"

I nodded. "Yes, I can. And if you wanted to put it somewhere else …" My voice trailed off, as I couldn't for the life of me think where else I could tolerate it. Certainly not in our bedroom. And not in the study either—not in the one room that didn't transmit constant reminders of its previous mistress. "How about the hall?" I said.

"I'll think about it," Joe said and, at that moment, I decided not to tell him about my morning, or about those damned figurines. Somehow I didn't think he would believe me.

Chapter Three

"What a lovely scent," Diane said as she came into the hall.

"I can't smell anything," I said.

"No, it's distinctive. I'll get it in a minute." She handed over her umbrella and I put it in the stand next to the front door. Emily again. She thought of everything. Including where to put guests' dripping umbrellas, and even *that* receptacle was an antique.

"Have you been here before?" I asked, as I led Diane past the living room and closed study door, where Joe was slaving away over a hot computer.

"Only a couple of times. Joe and I were on the same Community Hall committee. I inherited *that* post from my predecessor and Joe landed it when he became the local GP, so that's how I knew him. But Emily never invited me to any of her swish parties, so I only came here when it was Joe's turn to host the meeting. We used to congregate in the kitchen, so I don't remember ever being in any of the other rooms."

In the kitchen, I had brewed a cafetière of strong French coffee.

"Another fabulous smell," Diane said, smiling as she sat at the table.

I poured coffee and set hers in front of her. "Do you know anything about this house? I mean, are there any local legends I should know about?"

"Sorry, I don't follow you."

I took a deep breath and a gulp of hot, black coffee. "I had the oddest experience here on the morning of the day I phoned you."

"Sorry I had to dash off like that. I thought you sounded a bit fraught. Something about an attic and a chair?"

I shrugged, trying to appear nonchalant, but my muscles tensed as I spoke. "I wondered if anyone had ever mentioned the possibility that this house might be haunted." I held my breath and waited for her to burst out laughing. She didn't.

She looked at me intently and spoke. "Got it. Vanilla. That smell in the hall? Vanilla. Emily's favorite I believe. I remember that I remarked on it once, when I came for a meeting. Joe told me that she used to spray all the rooms with it." She paused and studied my face for a moment. "You've gone very pale. What is it?"

"That's what I smelled in that room. The room where I had the experience."

"If the room had been shut up for a long time, maybe it lingered."

I shook my head. "No, it would have faded long ago. Besides, that doesn't explain why you smelled it so strongly in the hall."

Diane looked thoughtful for a few seconds. "Well, all I remember is that I associate vanilla with Emily. That probably doesn't help a lot, though, does it?"

I did my best to smile but I'm sure all I achieved was, at best, a wobbly effort.

"Funnily enough," I said, "I would have thought the scent of roses was more her style. Joe told me Emily loved roses. Especially cream-colored ones, like the one in that photograph in the living room." Then I remembered. "Of course, you won't have seen it. I'll show you."

She followed me and I pointed to the portrait, which still leant against the wall.

Diane went over to it and picked it up, wincing at the weight of the frame. She looked at it for a moment and nodded. "That's the Emily I remember all right. She could have been a model, you know. She would have earned a fortune. But that probably wouldn't have suited her. I rather think modeling would have been somewhat beneath her." She replaced the photograph where she had found it. "Bugger!" She sucked her right forefinger.

"What is it?"

"Must have caught it on a sharp bit of the frame." She examined the injured finger. "Drew blood as well."

"I'm so sorry. Shall I get you a bandage?"

Diane smiled and wound a tissue around her finger. "No, I'll be fine thanks. Just a pinprick. Nothing serious."

"I'll get Joe to look at that frame. Maybe it got damaged when it fell."

"I expect so. It's very heavy. A fall like that couldn't have done it any good. Shouldn't think Emily would have liked it much either." She laughed.

"You didn't like her very much, did you?"

Diane screwed up her face. "Can't say I have much time for her sort of woman."

"What sort is that?"

"Oh, the type who live off their husband's money and lounge around all day. To salve their consciences, they go off and do some high profile good works, bask in the resulting lavish praise, and trot off for their second pedicure of the week."

"Well, I'm afraid you'll be disappointed in me because, right now, I'm living off my husband's money, not doing any good works and not going for any pedicures."

"Ah, but you see the difference is you're not comfortable with this situation, are you?"

I thought for a moment. "No, not really. I'd rather have a job."

"Precisely. So if I were you, I'd start looking for one. Even if it's part time. It'll do wonders for your self-confidence."

Diane was certainly perceptive—and refreshingly forthright. I would always know where I stood with her. Such a welcome change from the false smiles of the old biddies.

She continued. "I'm afraid I haven't heard any stories about this house. I know it's old. Victorian I believe."

I nodded. "The top floor looks as if it provided the servant accommodation and also the nursery. I had my weird experience in one of those rooms."

I told Diane what I thought I must have imagined.

"Whew, that's some detail for a mind game," she said. "Can we go up? I'd love to go into that room."

My stomach jellied and I felt sick. "I don't know if ... I mean, I know I must have imagined it, but the thought of going up there again fills me with horror."

"But you were alone last time. This time you've got me by your side and I'm a match for any ghost."

Was she making fun of me? I decided not. If anything, she seemed to be trying to reassure me.

"Very well, I'll take you up there. But not a word to Joe. He knows nothing about it."

"I'd like to say hello before I go, if that's OK."

"That's fine. When we come back down."

I led her up the stairs to the top floor.

"That smell of vanilla is really strong up here, isn't it?" Diane said, wrinkling her nose. "Almost too strong."

I sniffed the air. "I smelled it up here the other day, but I'm not getting anything now."

"Come on, show me that room. I'm dying to see it."

My heart pounded as I neared the door. With trembling fingers, I grasped the handle and turned it. As before, the door opened easily. The earlier shower had passed and sun streamed through the windows. We stepped inside.

"So that's the famous chair?" Diane crossed the room and touched it. "Emily would have almost certainly used this, not long before she died, I would have thought. Has Joe not mentioned it to you?"

"To be honest, I haven't told him any of this. I knew I couldn't casually mention finding this room and the chair without blurting everything out. We've had a couple of arguments about Emily lately and I didn't want to run the risk of starting another one."

"Still a sore point, is she?"

I nodded.

"It can't have been easy for him. At the end."

I was curious. Joe had never gone into any detail about Emily's final illness, only that she had suffered from cancer of the esophagus. He had clearly found it painful to talk about it and I had no wish to cause him further grief over something which, it could be argued, was really none of my business. But Diane seemed to know something and this was too good an opportunity to miss. Besides, it might help me understand Joe's continued heartache better.

"What happened … in the end?"

Diane sat down on the chair and I held my breath, certain at any moment it would grab her. But she seemed OK. Relaxed and comfortable, even. I realized I was still holding my breath and I released it.

There was nowhere for me to sit, so I stood and listened.

"Cancer of the esophagus is particularly nasty. My Aunt Susan had it. By the time she died, she was little more than a shriveled, bald skeleton. In Emily's case, I don't know what she looked like. For the last three months of her life, no one saw her but Joe and various doctors. She had twenty-four-hour care at home.

"So she actually died in this house? I didn't know."

"Oh yes, she died in her own bed."

I shivered and bile rose up inside me. Surely Joe and I weren't sleeping in the same bed where his first wife had died? The thought was too macabre and I would definitely have to find a way of tackling that with him. I'd never sleep soundly again until I did.

Diane frowned. "Are you all right? Didn't you know any of this?"

I shook my head. "I could tell Joe found it painful to talk about and I didn't like to pry. You're the only person I feel I can ask."

"I'm not much help, I'm afraid."

"But at least you were in the village at the time. You say no one saw her for the last three months? What was she like immediately before that?"

"The last time I saw her was at some fundraiser in the Community Hall. She was looking thinner and a little gaunt, but still beautiful, and I got the impression she was wearing a rather expensive wig. The color was identical to her own hair but … well, you know, there's often something about a wig. Doesn't look entirely natural."

"So she would have had some chemo by then?"

"Undoubtedly, if my aunt's experience was anything to go by. She died seven years ago, so I don't think much would have changed in the twelve months between her death and Emily's diagnosis. I remember the old biddies bustling around, clucking like mother hens. I think it irritated Emily a bit because she snapped at Mrs. Hope-Collins. I'd never seen that before. Emily was always so gracious. So gracious in fact that it used to make me feel sick. Didn't the woman possess any temper at all?" Diane raised her eyes to heaven and hoisted herself out of the chair.

"Nice mirror," she said, pointing at it. "Shame to tuck it away up here, but then, that's another bit of Emily isn't it? Ever thought of redecorating and exorcising her completely?"

Had I? I laughed. "You wouldn't believe how much I want to do that. Joe won't hear of it."

"You'll have to work on him."

I knew she was right. She strolled past me and I followed her, closing the door behind us.

Only then did I remember. When I had left that room three days earlier, the chair had been fully raised and tilted. No one had been in there until Diane and I today. So how had the chair returned to its normal upright position?

"Whatever is it, Chrissie? You look as if you've seen a ghost."

I felt lost and suddenly, terribly alone. Here was this woman I barely knew, and right now she was my only friend. My sister, Roni, was the other side of the world, in Melbourne. My old library friends had been more like acquaintances and, since meeting Joe and falling in love with him, I had tended to let other friendships slide. I had become so wrapped up in him and now, in the house I shared with him, I felt vulnerable and afraid.

Diane held my arm and steered me downstairs, treating me like some sort of fragile object that, at any moment, might fall and smash itself into tiny pieces.

She set me down on the sofa in the living room and made for the drinks cabinet.

Before I could protest, a large brandy was thrust into my hand.

"Take a swig and tell me what happened."

I looked up at her, nodded, drank and coughed as the strong liquid hit the back of my throat.

"Better?" she asked.

I nodded and told her about the chair. "I'm sorry, it's just that no one has been in that room since I was last there and it couldn't have righted itself, could it?"

Diane frowned. "I must admit, I don't see how, but maybe Joe went up there and didn't mention it. Maybe *he* put it straight. Why not ask him?"

I had my doubts, but pasted a smile on my face and nodded. "You're right. That's a good idea."

In the end, we decided not to disturb Joe, and Diane left shortly after. As I closed the front door behind her, I debated whether to trouble him with my concerns, but the study door was still firmly closed and I decided another hour or so wouldn't make any difference.

A wave of tiredness washed over me. I hadn't slept too well the past couple of nights. Maybe a nap would help? I debated going up to bed but, in the light of what Diane had told me, I couldn't face lying down on a bed where Emily might have drawn her last breath. I settled for the comfier of the two sofas in the living room and curled up, drifting off to sleep almost immediately.

I awoke to a smiling Joe handing me a cup of tea.

"Hello, sleepyhead."

I sat up and rubbed my eyes. "What time is it?"

"Just after four."

"Good grief, I must have been asleep for three hours or more."

"In that case, you must have needed it. Here's your tea. That'll perk you up."

I accepted it from him. "Thanks." I loved Joe's tea. He always made it good and strong.

He sat on a nearby chair and crossed his legs.

"Did you get everything done?" I asked.

He nodded. "Yes, I've had a very productive day all in all and I think I should take my wife out for a meal tonight to round it all off. What do you think? Fancy an Italian?"

My favorite. "Sounds lovely."

"That's settled. I'll ring them in a minute and book us in."

"Joe?"

"Yes?"

I gathered my courage and took a deep breath. "I've been up in the attic for the first time, this week."

His eyes widened but the smile remained. "Oh yes. What did you make of all the rubbish up there? Emily always intended to sort it all out but she never quite got around to it. Think you'll give it a go?"

"I'd like to certainly, but one of the rooms is a bit ... odd, isn't it?"

"Odd? How do you mean? Which room?"

"The one with the freestanding mirror and the Churchill chair."

"Chair? Oh, yes, the orthopedic chair. How is it odd then? It's one of the emptiest if I remember. That's why I put the chair there, out of the way."

"However did you get it up the stairs?"

"Sheer determination, brute force, and a helping hand from Sam Hope-Collins. You know Gladys?"

"Yes."

"Her son. Nice chap, lives in Manchester but was down here one weekend to visit his parents and offered to help."

"So whose chair was it? Emily's?"

Joe's face clouded over and the smile vanished. "Yes. Anyway, it's just a chair. Didn't fit in with the rest of the furniture down here. It was no longer needed, so up it went. It'll be a good idea to hang onto it though. You never know when it might come in handy."

I was determined to pursue this. "Diane Sterling came over this morning. She sent her best wishes. We didn't like to disturb you."

The smile returned, as if it had never been gone. Relief, maybe, that I had changed the subject and saved him the trouble.

"I thought I heard the door. Deep in concentration I'm afraid. I should have come out and greeted her. I hope she won't think I was being rude."

"I think she understood you were busy. She's a teacher, after all, so she needs to be able to shut the door on the world and concentrate too."

"True enough. I'm glad you're starting to make friends here. It can't be easy for you, with no work colleagues and being in a strange place."

"With some strange people," I said.

"Yes, well one or two of them are a bit eccentric."

"And lost somewhere in the mid-twentieth century."

Joe laughed. "You're probably right. Anyway, what did you two talk about?"

I took a deep breath. "A few things. The house. People in the village. Emily …"

He tensed. His face froze. I know I didn't imagine it and his next words confirmed my suspicions. "Why on earth would you discuss Emily? Diane hardly knew her." The edge to his voice sliced through the air.

Another deep breath. "She said Emily died in this house. In bed. Is that our bed?"

Joe sprang to his feet. "What if she did? What the hell business is that of yours? And what has it got to do with Diane? Is that all you have to do? Gossip about a woman who isn't here to defend herself?"

"*Defend* herself? Why would she need to do that?"

"In my experience when women start gossiping, nothing good comes from it. They're certainly not looking to enhance anyone's reputation. More likely to wreck it."

"Oh don't be stupid. Joe. We weren't wrecking her reputation. Some strange things have happened to me in this house and I didn't want to upset you with them. Suffice it to say, Emily still manages to maintain her presence pretty much all over this place."

Joe's voice rose to match mine, yet he missed the point entirely. "Don't start all that again. This house doesn't need redecorating and that's an end to it. If you want to redecorate anywhere, do the attic. Leave everything else as it is."

"Including having her photograph staring down at me, I suppose." I glanced over to where the portrait should have been resting on the floor, only to find it no longer there.

Sure enough, it hung back on the wall. My heart plummeted.

"When did you re-hang it?"

"While you were asleep. The hook needed to be pushed back in. It's perfectly firm. Can't understand why it fell down in the first place."

The inference was obvious. "I didn't take it down. It fell."

"Strange the glass didn't break."

"Yes it is, isn't it? But a lot of strange things happen in this house. Not that you're aware of it of course." My anger rose and something clicked in my brain. If this continued, I knew I wouldn't be able to restrain myself from letting all my pent-up anger and frustration, not to mention my fears, pour out all over him.

"*Now* what are you talking about?" he said.

"I'm talking about the attic. That bloody chair has got a mind of its own. I sat in it and it started to rise and tilt as if it were plugged in, only it wasn't. And the mirror …"

His expression stopped me. He might have been staring at a total stranger. "Chrissie. I can't begin to understand what you're talking about. Upstairs in the attic is a room with a chair, a mirror, and some boxes of old paperbacks that really belong in a charity shop. In fact let's go up there. Now."

He grabbed my unwilling hand and half dragged me from the room.

"Joe, no, please. I don't want to go up there again." My eyes filled with tears. I wanted to be almost anywhere rather than where I was right now. But he wasn't going to release me until he had accomplished his objective.

I stumbled up the stairs behind him, and I felt his grip tightening on my hand, crushing my fingers.

At the top of the house, he wrenched open the door and shoved me in. His eyes frightened me. They were wild, as if he didn't see me at all.

The chair stood in front of the mirror. Just as Diane and I had left it.

"Sit down. *Go on.*" He thrust me forward.

"No, Joe. I don't want to."

"You will sit in that chair."

He lifted me up with a roughness I had never experienced before. Where had my Joe gone? The man in the room with me was barely recognizable. I struggled but he was too strong. He pushed me down into the chair, gripping my arms so I couldn't escape.

"See? It's just an ordinary chair. There are no electric sockets in this room, so it can't possibly move."

Tears were misting my eyes, so I couldn't see properly. Memories stirred in my mind. Horrible memories that I didn't permit myself anymore. My childhood. My father. "*Please* Joe. Let me go. What's got into you?"

Suddenly, he relaxed his hold and I regained the use of my hands. I brushed away the tears from my eyes and watched him back away, a shocked expression on his face.

"God, Chrissie, I'm so sorry. I don't know … what are we doing in here anyway? We were downstairs."

"You dragged me up here, remember?"

He stared at me, as if trying to recall.

I leapt up, eager to get away from that chair. I avoided the mirror too, scared of what I might see there, after the last time.

Joe rubbed his forehead and seemed to be trying to make sense of his actions. "I remember being downstairs. We were arguing over Emily's photograph. You said something about this room. I don't remember anything after that. Not until I realized I was holding you down in that chair."

"You seemed like a stranger. As if something possessed you."

"That *is* crazy. No, I've been working too hard, that's all. I'll take the rest of the weekend off and get some sleep. But can we postpone dinner tonight? I don't really feel like it."

"Me neither," I said, as I edged closer to the door.

Joe touched the frame of the mirror. "She used to have this in the bedroom. Emily always checked her appearance before she went anywhere, making sure her hemline was straight and she had no snags in her tights, checking that her jewelry was perfect for the occasion …"

He seemed to have drifted into a world of his own. Despite my desire to escape that awful room, I went up to him. He was standing in front of the mirror. I moved up close and glanced at his expression in the reflection.

My breath caught in my throat. In the mirror, I saw Joe, his face troubled. Standing at his shoulder was a smiling Emily. The scent of vanilla filled my nostrils.

It followed me as I screamed and raced from the room, down the stairs and out of the front door, where I clung to one of the pillars, trying to catch my breath. Anyone seeing me would have thought I was mad, or ill, but there was a courtyard and a path between me and the gates and we were on a quiet country lane with little traffic. I was alone.

Chapter Four

The sun shone in the late afternoon and a gentle breeze soothed me. My breathing returned to normal after a few minutes, and at last I let go of the pillar, confident that I wouldn't pass out. The front door was wide open but I was too scared to cross the threshold. I don't know how many minutes I stood there before Joe appeared, his forehead creased with worry.

"Chrissie whatever's the matter?"

"You took your time, didn't you?"

"What? I came straight down after you."

"No you didn't. I've been here for ages." I glanced at my watch, which was no help at all, as I had no idea when I had rushed out there. "Did you enjoy seeing her again?"

"Seeing who? What are you talking about?"

"I saw her in the mirror. Emily."

Joe raised his eyes skywards. "For heaven's sake, Chrissie. Listen to yourself. Emily's dead."

"Well I really wish you'd tell *her* that because it doesn't seem to have registered with her."

"This is crazy. Come inside. We can't stand here arguing on the doorstep, what will the neighbors think?"

"*Neighbors?* They're the least of my concerns." I was shaking, scared stiff of entering that house again. What would she try next?

Joe put his arm around me and gently led me back in and up the stairs. I was only half-aware of where we were headed, but as we moved into the bedroom, I froze.

"Joe, please tell me Emily didn't die in that bed."

He turned me to face him, his hands on my shoulders. "I promise you, Emily didn't die in that bed. I got rid of it after … I couldn't bear to sleep on it either. It brought back too many memories. In the end, she was so frail, the slightest movement caused her pain, so I moved into one of the spare rooms. The cancer spread to her bones, you see."

"She must have really suffered," I said, my voice thick with emotion. All my fears suddenly seemed ridiculous in the face of his grief. "I'm so sorry."

"You didn't know. I've never spoken about it to anyone before." He paused and drew a deep breath. "Even though they increased the morphine, she was in terrible pain. She faded in front of my eyes." Tears spilled over and coursed down his cheeks. "I lost my Emily weeks before she died. In the end, she was so drugged up she didn't know who I was. Maybe she didn't even know who *she* was. But, right to the end, she was determined to die in this house."

"She knew she was dying?"

"Yes. Emily knew everything all along. Right from the first diagnosis, she insisted on being kept fully informed about her condition and the ongoing prognoses. If she thought anyone was keeping anything from her, she wouldn't let it go. She had to know. She said it gave her back some kind of control."

I stroked his hair. If only he had told me this months ago, weeks, days even. But I could see how hard it was for him, I felt so guilty for forcing him into this.

"I didn't mean to upset you, Joe. I really hope you know that. I needed to know. To help me understand."

He stroked my cheek and managed a weak smile. His voice was soft. My Joe was back. "I know, my love. It can't be easy being my second wife."

"Emily's a tough act to follow."

Joe nodded and the smile grew stronger. "You're doing a grand job." He kissed the tip of my nose and drew me closer. I nestled into his chest and felt more at peace than I had for days.

If only it could have lasted.

The next few weeks passed peacefully enough. I saw Diane around once a week for coffee or the occasional pizza. Before I knew where we were, summer had passed and the leaves were turning golden, russet, red and brown and fell from the trees. The gardener needed his vacuum every weekly visit, and sack upon sack of dead leaves from the sycamores and beech trees in our garden stacked up, ready for collection.

The nights drew in, the clocks went back, and the central heating went on. Skimpy summer dresses were replaced with chunky sweaters and winter coats, and the hearth in the living room blazed with a log fire most evenings. I much preferred it to coal—Emily's preferred fuel. The scent of applewood permeated the house and I realized I hadn't smelled vanilla since that tumultuous afternoon two months earlier.

I didn't venture back up to the attic. After all, if Emily hadn't needed to go up there in most of the eight years she lived here, why would I? Since Joe had poured his heart out to me, my feelings about her had changed. With no further scary incidents to worry about, I felt pity, rather than fear, when I thought of her. After all, the poor woman had gone through hell at the end. And poor Joe had been forced to stand by and watch the woman he loved deteriorate, knowing he could do nothing to help her.

I didn't even mind too much about her portrait anymore. I tried to avoid looking at it.

In mid-December, with late Christmas shopping in mind, I met up with Diane after school. We sipped coffee in the local café and shared holiday plans.

"I'm staying with my parents in London," she said. "There'll be ten of us for Christmas Day. Should just make it to the King's speech before war breaks out. My father's an ardent Royalist and my two brothers are republicans, so you can imagine what happens when Dad calls for silence to listen to him. He used to insist we stood for the National Anthem but since his gout got worse, that's gone by the board."

I giggled. "Sounds like an eventful afternoon. We're going to be quiet this year. I have a party I'm dreading on Boxing Day though. Apparently Emily set up a tradition of asking the biddies and the rest of the neighbors over for sherry and mince pies in the morning. After she died, Joe carried it on, so guess who can't wriggle out of hostess duty?"

"Oh God, how awful."

"Have to grin and bear it I suppose. Still, apparently they only stay for a couple of hours and decamp to the vicar's for cold cuts and wine. Fortunately, because we've already done our hosting bit, we get to abstain from that. Washing up to do, you see."

"I thought you had a machine for that?" She winked.

"We do. But they don't need to know that, do they?"

"Still you'll have quite a houseful while they are there."

"Around thirty I should think. Some of them may have to stand, but people like to do that, don't they? Mingle, wander around. Stare admiringly at Emily's photograph."

"Does that still bother you?"

I shook my head. "Not really."

"You're more tolerant than I would be."

I shrugged. "As long as Joe and I are happy, that's really all I care about. And we are. Things have been great since we had that talk."

"I'm glad."

"And I think I must have been a bit overwrought. Maybe the result of moving into a house where such a strong personality lived."

"You're probably right." Diane glanced at her watch. "We'd better get on if we're going to get our shopping done. I know the Woolton Center's open late tonight but it's after five."

———

I found beautiful red and gold tree decorations, which were perfect for my needs as I certainly wasn't going to hang Emily's. And I found a lovely soft leather wallet for Joe. I had noticed his old one had become tatty and worn. This one was a bit expensive, but he was worth it and I was sure he'd love it.

Diane and I wouldn't see each other again before the holidays, so we hugged and wished each other Happy Christmas before going in our separate directions.

I remember humming "Deck the Halls" as I turned the key in the lock. Warm air, scented with applewood, met me in the hall. I closed and bolted the door behind me as usual.

"Joe?" I called. No answer. He must be in though, or else the fire wouldn't have been lit.

I took off my coat and hung it in the hall closet, removed my boots, slipped my feet into cozy slippers and padded into the living room. All the lamps were on, but not the main light. It gave the room a warm glow, accentuated by the blazing, crackling fire.

I looked around the room. No sign of Joe. I was about to go in search of him elsewhere when something caught my eye. Something that shouldn't have been there.

I reached for the main light, switched it on, and stared in disbelief. There, through the archway, facing Emily's portrait, stood the chair from the attic.

"*No!*"

Joe was there in an instant. "Hi, darling."

I ignored his greeting and pointed to the chair. "What the hell is that doing down here?"

"We're going to have a lot of guests on Boxing Day, so I thought it would help with seating."

I turned on him. "How did you get it down here?"

"Good old Sam Hope-Collins. He's here for the holidays, staying with his parents, and I bumped into him at the surgery today. He'd come to collect a prescription for his father. The old man has a bit of difficulty getting in and out of normal chairs these days and he told me they'd bought one of these. One thing led to another and I asked him to come and help me lug it downstairs. His father will be able to sit in it when they come here for drinks."

"No," I said. "He won't be able to sit in it because it isn't going to be here." I wasn't going to be deterred by Joe's shocked expression.

"I'm sorry, Joe, but that thing isn't staying in this room. There's something wrong with it. Something … unnatural."

To my horror, Joe's expression turned to one of contemptuous anger. "Don't be so ridiculous. A chair can't be unnatural. That bloody imagination of yours is working overtime again. The chair stays."

He strode off into the study and slammed the door. I burst into tears and raced up to our bedroom.

I lay on the bed, devastated. How could everything turn sour so quickly? For weeks I had been happy. I had even started a tentative search for a part-time job. I planned interesting meals for Joe and our sex life had never been more fulfilling. When I came home and opened that living room door, I was enjoying my life. And now …

I lay in the dark and pulled the duvet around me, as the outside temperature dropped toward freezing. The bedroom had grown quite chilly too, but I was worn out, so I closed my eyes and started to drift.

Something wrenched me from sleep. I sat bolt upright and reached for the lamp. I clicked the switch but nothing happened. The scent of vanilla filled the room. I clicked again but the bulb sputtered and went out.

The bedroom door slammed.

"Joe?" I called into the black void.

I heard a rustle and the vanilla grew stronger.

I gripped the duvet tighter, right up to my chin. I hardly dared breathe. My gut twisted as I realized something—or someone—was tugging the duvet from the bottom of the bed. I pulled hard. It pulled harder. I could feel the duvet slip through my fingers. Fear shot through my body and chilled me to the core. I heard whimpering. It took me a moment to realize it was me.

The duvet was whipped off and an icy blast hit me. The smell of vanilla was overpowering. Its cloying sweetness made me gag.

"Who are you? What do you want?" I cried. "Emily?"

Sharp nails raked my hands, and powerful fingers tightened around my wrists, pulling me off the bed. I screamed.

"*Joe.* Help me!"

The whispering started—a woman's voice, but I couldn't make out the words. My assailant tossed me back and forth like a rag doll, gripping my wrists so tightly I thought they would break. Again and again I screamed. I pleaded for mercy. The heavy velvet curtains blocked out all light and I had no idea what was fighting me. Only that it wasn't Joe.

Suddenly, light flooded the room from the overhead bulb and I was released. I fell onto the rug, tears streaming down my face as Joe rushed over to me.

"What the hell happened? Did you have a nightmare?"

"A nightmare?" I sobbed and held out my arms. "What nightmare does this?"

Joe stared at my hands. "Does what? I can't see anything."

Still sobbing, I peered down at my hands. I turned them over, remembering the pain of those sharp nails, raking off the skin. But there were no scratches, no blood. I examined my wrists, certain they should show livid bruises, wondering why they no longer hurt. They were unmarked. There was nothing to show they had ever been in that grip so tight it cut off the circulation.

Joe was right. I must have fallen asleep and had the mother and father of all nightmares.

"But it was so real. And the lamp … the bulb blew."

Joe pressed the switch and the bedside light came on. I stared at him.

"I don't understand."

Joe lifted me up and put his arms around me. "My fault. I should have consulted you about that chair. I don't understand why it bothers you so much. But if you really want it moved back, I'll see if Sam can come over again. Not sure quite how I'll explain it though."

I sighed, desperate to regain my senses. I had just had a nightmare, I told myself. None of it had been real. "No, you're right. I'm being stupid. Leave it there until after Boxing Day and then move it back. That way everyone's happy."

"Sure?" he asked.

"Sure," I said, sounding far more confident than I felt.

Chapter Five

For the next ten days, I avoided spending any time at all in that part of the room. We spent our first Christmas Day together alone, enjoying each other's company and, all too soon, Boxing Day dawned and I laid out sherry glasses and warmed mince pies.

"You've done a grand job with these." Joe selected a freshly baked pie from the cooling tray and took a bite out of it.

"Hey," I said, as I smacked him with the tea towel. "Those are for later."

"Just testing. For someone who's never baked before, you've got a very light touch. This pastry melts in your mouth. Delicious."

I only just managed to stop myself from asking how they compared with Emily's.

Joe grabbed another mince pie and laughed. Laughing with him, I chased him out of the kitchen as the doorbell rang and the first of our guests arrived.

"Mrs. Hope-Collins, what a pleasure," I heard him say and offered up a silent prayer to help me get through the next two hours.

Mr. Hope-Collins settled himself in the orthopedic chair and I waited on him with a seemingly endless succession of mince pies and top-ups of sherry. I even debated leaving a bottle with him, but decided that would incur the wrath of the ever-watchful Gladys. He sat comfortably, even nodding off at one point. Clearly the chair had no quarrel with him.

I circulated among my guests and tried to ignore the poorly disguised stares and remarks made behind hands. How was I faring in comparison to Emily? Not well, I feared, although my mince pies seemed to be meeting with approval. At twelve thirty I ran out of them completely, so out came my Christmas cake. That disappeared within fifteen minutes.

The sherry held up well, but with no sign of anything else appearing from the kitchen, our guests gradually drained their glasses, thanked Joe, nodded at me and left in pairs.

At one fifteen, Joe closed the door on the last of them and I breathed again.

He held his arms out to me. "Come here," he said, and I went to him. "You did a great job, Chrissie. I only wish they were more accepting."

"So do I. I mean, they're not rude as such. Well, not to my face anyway. But it's the snide comments and the constant feeling of being unfavorably compared to Emily."

"It must hurt. Especially when you've gone to as much trouble as you have."

"Well at least you appreciate it."

"No one could have done better."

"Not even Emily?" The words were out before I could check them.

I held my breath during the pause that followed, until he spoke. "Not even Emily," he said, at last. And I breathed again.

He took my hand and led me up to bed and when we made love, his touch was tender, his kisses warm and caressing.

The room was lit by a single bedside lamp, casting his face into shadow as he moved on top of me. His fingers stroked my face and he bent to kiss me. I returned his kisses with passion. In our blissful lovemaking, all my fears seemed to melt away and become irrelevant. Nonsensical even.

We moved together, rising to climax at the same time. Joined as one. I cried out and he echoed me before collapsing on top of me, panting. Our hearts raced.

I heard him murmur and I almost smiled. I would have too, if only I hadn't been so sure of what I heard.

"Willow ..."

More like a breath than a whisper. The nickname he had said he hated hung in the air between us. Tears streamed down my cheeks.

The day after Boxing Day, Joe was back at work and I was alone in the house once more. Mary was staying with her family in Norfolk for the holidays, so I busied myself with cleaning and tidying the house. Anything to take my mind off what I had heard last night, in bed.

The living room especially needed sorting out and I polished furniture and ornaments, dusted pictures, fluffed up cushions, vacuumed, and realized I had avoided the area around the chair and Emily's portrait. Telling myself not to be so stupid, I marched through the archway. Emily gazed down at me as usual. I raised my duster — only to have it knocked out of my hand.

I cried out as an excruciating grip bit into my wrists. I stared down at them. My hands were white, bloodless. I was losing feeling in the ends of my fingers.

I looked up at the portrait and flinched. I knew it couldn't, but surely her expression had changed. Sheer malevolence stared down at me.

I heard an animal roar and was thrown across the room, landing painfully on the floor and banging my shoulder on a bookcase.

"What do you want?" I cried.

A vase smashed against the wall to my right and showered me with shards of porcelain. I screamed as the heavy velvet curtains were ripped from the window. A shadow darted across my field of vision and I struggled to stand, only to be pushed over again.

Blows rained down on my body. I closed my eyes and curled myself into a fetal position, my arms shielding my head as I yelled for it to stop. But still the invisible blows rained down on me.

"You're nothing. Less than nothing. You'll never be any good. Never. You're worthless."

I felt the words rather than heard them and they sent my mind roaring back to my childhood. It was no longer Emily, or some nameless poltergeist, but my father's voice. And I felt my father's hands pull me up off the floor and shake me back and forth till I was sure my bones would crack.

"No, please stop. Stop, Daddy. *Please*. You're *hurting* me!" My little girl voice sounded shrill and unfamiliar to my ears. How many times had he done this to me? How many other times had I cowered in the cupboard under the stairs, too scared to come out, while my sister Roni screamed for mercy and my mother lay unconscious, where he had knocked her out.

But Daddy was dead. Twenty years had passed since Roni and I had offered silent prayers of thanksgiving as we linked arms with our mother at his graveside. Such a feeling of release. Of freedom.

How could he be back?

Sharp, ringing slaps stung my cheeks.

"You no good brat. I'll teach you a lesson you'll never forget."

I screamed. In the distance, the doorbell rang.

The blows stopped. The voice stopped. I sank to the floor, my eyes shut tight.

The doorbell rang again, more urgently this time, and someone hammered on the door. I struggled to my feet and opened my eyes. Stared in disbelief. Where there should have been devastation, all was neat and tidy.

I was aware of my wrists throbbing. As I limped to the door, I saw bruises on my arms and, as I opened the door, I watched them disappear.

Diane's pale, anxious face greeted me, along with a blast of icy air. Frost lay thick on the ground, so at least I knew the chill was natural.

"Whatever's the matter? I heard you screaming."

I opened the door wider to let her in and burst into tears.

"Come on, let's get you sat down. God, you're shaking."

I knew I was. Shock had set every muscle trembling and I could barely walk. Diane guided me into the kitchen. I couldn't face the living room at that moment. I sat at the table, trying to collect my thoughts, while she put the kettle on and made us mugs of instant coffee.

She set mine in front of me. "Drink that. I've made it nice and strong."

I looked up at her. "Thanks."

She sat opposite me. "Tell me what happened."

I told her, and hesitated as I recalled the extraordinary sequence of events. I realized how crazy I must sound, especially as nothing in that living room would support my story.

"Let me see your hands," she said. I held them out to her, turned them over, and pulled up the sleeves of my sweater so she could see my wrists and forearms. Not one mark to show the pain I had felt so shortly before.

"This is so weird," she said. "Come on, let's go into the living room."

I flinched. "No, I'd really rather not go there."

"You're with me," she said. "Nothing's going to happen while I'm around."

Still unsure, I stood on wobbly feet and followed her, hanging a few steps back until I had no choice but to enter that room.

Diane made straight for the archway. She must have realized I wasn't behind her and turned around. "There's nothing here. You're fine." She beckoned me and, reluctantly, I moved forward, sure at any moment I would be thrown backwards. But she was right. Nothing would happen while she was there. Nothing would happen while Joe was there. Only while I was alone.

My eyes traveled around the room and I forced myself to look up at Emily's photograph. Any change to her expression had gone. How I longed to tear that photograph from the wall and smash it to unrecognizable fragments. My hands even started to rise.

"Chrissie." Maybe Diane sensed what I was about to do. Her voice held a distinct note of warning in it. I lowered my hands.

I turned round to face her. Her look spoke volumes. She thought I had imagined it all.

"Where did you fall?" she asked.

I pointed. "Over there. I fell against that bookcase and hurt my shoulder." I rubbed it, expecting to feel the pain of a bruise. But, of course, I felt nothing.

"Does it hurt still?"

I shook my head. "No."

"Where did the vase smash?"

I pointed to a spot a couple of feet away from where I had lain. "Against the wall, next to where I fell."

Diane peered at the wall, no doubt looking for telltale marks. She crouched down. I prayed she would find a shard of porcelain. Anything to back up my story. She poked at the skirting board but came away empty-handed.

"There's nothing here now. Can you see the vase anywhere? What did it look like?"

In the midst of what had happened, I hadn't registered which of the room's handful of vases had so narrowly missed injuring me. I looked around but I couldn't see any missing.

I shook my head. "It's no good. I didn't see it properly. I was too scared and it all happened so quickly."

A fresh wave of tears overcame me and Diane put her arm around me. She led me back through the archway, over to the sofa, where I sat and clasped my head in my hands.

"Oh God, Diane, what's happening to me? I can't have imagined all this. I know I can't. What happened was real. As real as you being here and not believing me. You think I dreamed it all up somehow, don't you?"

Diane sighed. "It's not that. It's … well … I can't find any evidence to back up what you're saying. Surely the room couldn't right itself like that. There would be *something* to show for what you say you went through."

That did it. I jumped up. "What I *say* I went through? Have you any idea what it feels like to go through what I experienced this morning and not be believed? I thought you were my friend, Diane."

Diane stood too. "I am, Chrissie. Honestly I am. But you have to admit, if I had been the one to tell you all this, you would have had a pretty hard time digesting my story, wouldn't you?"

Of course, she was right. But it didn't help. I sat down again and stared at the empty grate. Diane sat too and we didn't speak for a few minutes.

I broke the uncomfortable silence. "Am I going out of my mind?"

Diane sighed. "No, but I do think you're overwrought. I also think, if I can be blunt, that you don't have enough to occupy your mind.

You're an intelligent woman, Chrissie, and until a few months ago, baking cakes wouldn't have satisfied you. But I saw how you were when you started making that Christmas cake and those mince pies. I felt I was watching *The Stepford Wives* all over again—and I don't mean the Bette Midler, comic version either."

That came as a shock. I had baked because that's what they expected of me. But, in a way, Diane had a point. I had enjoyed it and such activities had never before featured on my radar.

"I *have* been looking for a job," I said, hating how feeble I sounded.

She gave me a disbelieving stare. "Have you been looking, or has it been more of a quick glance? To salve your conscience? Has Joe told you not to look for one?"

"No, he would never try and stop me. In fact, he said if I wanted to get a job, he would support my decision."

"OK, how many jobs have you applied for, in total?"

I didn't like that question. I knew the answer and it didn't support my case. "Three. There haven't been many I was qualified to apply for locally."

"Three," Diane repeated. Her expression changed. I suppose I had become one of those women she so despised. When she spoke, her tone did nothing to dispel my suspicions. "Sorry, Chrissie, but if you want a job, you'll have to be a lot more active than that, and you'd better start soon too. You haven't enough to occupy your mind, so it's going off in all sorts of tangents of its own. You've had a frightening example of that today. You know, the human brain is capable of far more than we give it credit for, I'm convinced of that, so if you'll take my advice, you'll stop vegetating around here and start doing something about it."

Rage bubbled up inside me. How *dare* Diane criticize me like this? I'd only known her a few months. What right had she to tell me what to do?

"I resent that," I said, wanting to lash out at her, but I forced myself to leave it at that. Diane didn't believe me. She thought my mind had played tricks on me and the only one to blame was me. Idle, waste of space me.

"That's your choice." Diane's words were spiked with ice. She stood. "I've got to get back. Will you be all right?" There was no warmth in her question. Just duty.

If I'd said no, I don't know what she would have done. She so clearly wanted to get away. So I nodded.

"Stay there. I know the way out."

The note of finality was tangible. My only friend had dismissed me. She probably thought I was insane and she wouldn't be the last to think so.

I did as she suggested but, as soon as I heard the front door close, regretted it. I should have gone after her. Maybe I wasn't too late. But I heard her rev up her car engine and she was off down the drive before I could get out of the living room door.

I carried on walking, into the kitchen.

Chapter Six

Joe was called out on an emergency on New Year's Eve and I was left to see the New Year in alone. I raised my glass to Jools Holland on TV, sipped champagne and waited for my husband to come home. I wanted to call Diane and wish her a Happy New Year but didn't know what sort of reception I would get. In the end I sent her a text, but never received a reply.

The freezing dark weeks of January dragged on. Mary returned from her holiday and carried on the same as before. I tried to engage her in conversation, but she always seemed in a hurry to get away and carry on with her chores. In the end I gave up and settled for "Good morning," when she arrived and "Thanks, see you next time," when she left. I think she preferred it that way.

February brought snowstorms, hail, thunder, fog and gale force winds—almost everything the British weather could throw at us in fact, with the exception of sunshine.

My days were quiet. I stepped up the job-hunting for a while, but with nothing in the offing, my efforts began to slacken and I spent most of my time cooking, baking and reading. I became the local library's best customer. I might have liked to work there too, but they didn't have any job vacancies.

Despite Joe's constant assurances that he'd move it, the chair still stood in the living room, close to Emily's photograph. I avoided entering that part of the living room altogether.

I also avoided the attic until, one day, I finished my last book and wandered aimlessly around the house, tidying what didn't need tidying and rearranging what looked fine anyway. I had grown accustomed to Emily's fixtures and fittings and had stopped pestering Joe to let me redecorate. It simply wasn't worth the argument that inevitably followed.

Yes, I admit I had become a docile wife, but at least Joe and I were happy. Or I thought we were. Now I'll never know.

Valentine's Day was fast approaching and I bought Joe a beautiful card. An Art Deco couple gazed longingly into each other's eyes. There was no silly verse. Just a simple "Always and forever" inside. I also bought a bottle of his favorite Hugo Boss aftershave and wrapped it in fancy paper, tied with a red ribbon. I wanted our Valentine to be special.

Joe had to work of course, but before he left the doorbell rang and a dozen red roses arranged in a bouquet were placed in my arms.

I had, I'm sure, a silly grin on my face and heard the delivery girl's laughter as she returned to her van.

"They're beautiful, Joe, thank you."

"You're worth it, my angel." He kissed me warmly on the lips. "Now, smell me. Am I irresistible?"

I laughed and sniffed his neck. "I love that aftershave, but you'd better not be too irresistible. You're spoken for, remember?"

He laughed and opened the door. "I'll remember. Don't you worry. See you around six."

"Steak Diane for dinner."

He licked his lips. "Can't wait. Looking forward to dessert too."

"Apple pie."

"That's not what I meant."

I knew it. I waved him off and shut the door, locking and bolting it as I always did when I was alone. Even in a backwater like Thornton Waterville, you couldn't be too careful.

In the kitchen, I arranged my lovely flowers and took the vase into the living room, taking care to place it well away from the archway, the photograph and that chair.

The house was quiet. Mary wasn't due today and I had nothing planned, with the exception of dinner later. I looked at the pile of six books on the hall table, waiting for me to return them to the library.

In the utility room, I piled washing into the machine and switched it on. The rest of the morning was spent pottering around, doing things that didn't really demand my attention. Before I knew it, I looked at my watch. Lunchtime. I would take the books back this afternoon. But, with a sinking feeling, I realized that this was the afternoon the library shut. And I had no more books to read.

Panic set in. However crazy it might seem, I simply couldn't get through the day, not even a happy one like this, without my couple of hours curled up with Patricia Cornwell or John Grisham.

What should I do? The nearest bookshop was ten miles away and the buses ran hourly at this time of day. There would be no time to get there, select a book, catch the next bus back, and be home in time to prepare the three-course meal I had in mind.

I thought of those boxes of paperbacks in the attic. There would be something there, in my own house, that I could read. If only I could bring myself to go back up there.

I paced around the kitchen and told myself not to be such a wimp. I reminded myself that the accursed chair was in the living room. It could hardly trap me from there. Besides, it had been agreed that I had imagined all that, hadn't it? As Diane had said, my underemployed brain had played tricks on me.

Still I hesitated, but a quarter of an hour later I thumped my hand down on the table. Enough! I was going up there, I'd choose a book, come down, go into the living room and read the damn thing!

With a new resolve quickening my pace, I hurried up the stairs before I could change my mind. But at the top stair, I hesitated, not quite daring to step onto the landing.

I saw the closed door and took a deep breath before opening it. Inside, the dull winter light cast shadows in the corners. I ignored the mirror and focused on the nearest box of books. I upended it on the floor to speed up my search.

Emily must have had eclectic tastes in reading matter. Daniel Defoe nudged Jacqueline Susann, who gave way to P. D. James and Nora

Roberts. I turned over a battered copy of *Bleak House* and found an Armistead Maupin I hadn't read. I picked up *Maybe the Moon* and flicked the pages. Yes, that would definitely do. But, while I was there, I might as well see what else was on offer.

Gaining in confidence, I emptied the next box and the next and within minutes a small pile had turned into a larger one that would require a box of its own. I started to pile the books in and hoisted up the half-full box. I happened to glance over at the mirror and saw my reflection. A chill ran up and down my spine. Something had changed. I shouldn't have been able to see myself. Then I realized—the mirror had moved.

Certain that something was following me, I whimpered and escaped from the room, still clutching my box. Why I didn't drop it, I'll never know, but I was determined to keep hold of it. Hurrying made me jolt the box and my balance went haywire, but I had to get down those stairs and away from whatever was up there. I was halfway down the last flight when my awkward gait led to the inevitable and I tripped. The box flew out of my hands and crashed to the floor below. I nearly wrenched my arm out of its socket as I grabbed the banister, twisted and slid down onto my bottom. A breeze brushed past me, taking my breath away and I fainted.

———

I came to, still on the stairs, leaning against the banister. The light was fading, so I must have been there quite some time. I tried to stand and found my bottom hurt from where I had landed. My shoulder and upper arm ached and my head throbbed, but I finished my descent and picked up the scattered books, replacing them in the box.

I kept telling myself my imagination had been on overtime that afternoon. I put the box on the hall table and made my painful way into the kitchen.

As it turned out, there had been little point in my escapade. I had lost so much time that there would be none left for reading that afternoon. I had to prepare our Valentine's dinner.

We always ate in the kitchen and today would be no different, except for the candles of course. You must have candles on Valentine's

Day. Long, slender red ones. I found mine and placed two in small silver candlesticks on the table.

Over at the sink, I peeled potatoes for sautéing later. I had baked an apple pie the previous day, so I took that out of the fridge.

I debated whether or not to use our best cognac for the Diane sauce but decided that really was a bit too extravagant and settled for the cheaper alternative that I kept in one of the wall cabinets. Next, I washed the mangetout—Joe's favorite, although I wasn't too crazy about them myself.

Finally, with the steak trimmed and ready, and all the ingredients to hand, I allowed myself a satisfied smile, still fighting to suppress memories of the attic. Our first course would consist of a mushroom pâté I had made myself, accompanied by homemade Melba toasts. The champagne had been chilling for a couple of days and the glasses were next to it in the fridge.

I could do no more in the kitchen until Joe came home. Recently, his timekeeping had become a little erratic, owing to the pressures of work, so I was never sure, within half an hour or so, when he would open the door. He had said six, but that could easily stretch to half past. I wasn't going to risk overcooking his steak on Valentine's Day of all days.

I made my way upstairs and sank into a leisurely bath, reveling in the perfumed bubbles. I washed my hair and leaned back, sinking down into the silky water.

My new dress—purchased especially for today—was emerald green and fitted me as if it had been made specially for me. Its full skirt skimmed my knees and its tight waist accentuated my curves. With the diamond earrings Joe had bought me for my birthday glinting in my ears, I applied my makeup with extra care and studied my reflection in the dressing table mirror.

"You might not be the immaculate Emily," I said to my reflection. "But you don't scrub up too badly. Not today at any rate." I smiled and nodded to myself and slipped on a pair of strappy gold sandals.

In the back of my mind, I registered that today was also the sixth anniversary of Emily's death. I knew Joe's feelings must be mixed, to say the least.

At ten past six, I heard the scrape of the key in the lock. I jumped up from the kitchen table and ran to greet Joe in the hall. His smile was wide and his embrace warm and firm. "You look beautiful," he said. We kissed and I almost suggested we skip dinner, but he took my hand and led me into the living room, where I had the shock of my life.

"*What* the …" Joe dropped my hand as if it had burned him, while I stared incredulously at the devastation. Every single one of my beautiful red roses lay broken and crushed, as if someone had snapped them off and stamped on them, until they were almost flattened. Their glorious red hue stained the large cream rug on which they were scattered.

Joe bent and picked one up. He stared at it before thrusting it out to me. "Why, Chrissie?"

"No, Joe. I swear I didn't do this. How could I? It's so cruel. I *loved* those roses. I don't understand it. Who … what could have done this?"

Joe was having none of it. "Oh, come on, Chrissie. Who else has been here today? Diane? I thought you two weren't friends any longer."

I shook my head. "No one's been here but me, and I swear I didn't do this."

Joe's voice rose. "Then who in hell did?"

"In hell" was possibly more accurate than he knew. I knew it couldn't have been me. Not in my wildest imaginings. That left one other person. I pointed through the archway. It all seemed so clear to me now.

"Emily."

"*What?* That's sick, Chrissie. On today of all days, that is really sick." He stared at me as if I were a nasty taste in his mouth. At that moment, I felt as relevant to him as the hypodermic syringes he would have used and discarded today at his surgery.

He flung the battered rose away from him and strode out of the room, leaving me alone to clear up the mess. In the vase, twelve rose stems showed every sign of having been snipped, not torn as I had first guessed. Each bloom showed a clean cut, close to the head. I looked around but couldn't locate any scissors. Yet another mystery.

I knelt on the floor, surrounded by broken roses and wept till my eyes stung and no more tears would fall. A wave of righteous anger hit me and I struggled to my feet. I still ached from my earlier fall, but nothing was going to stop me confronting his first wife.

I marched through the archway and planted myself in front of her photograph.

"You *bitch*!" I said. "How *dare* you do this. How d*are* you. He's mine. Not yours. Do you hear me? *Mine.*" I heard an engine whir and I spun round. The chair was rising.

"Oh no you don't. Not this time. Because I'm ready for you. Do you hear me? You're not going to scare me again."

The door flew open and an angry-looking Joe stood there. "Who the hell are you shouting at? I can hear you in the study with the door shut."

My eyes flickered up at the photograph.

"Oh for heaven's sake, don't tell me you're shouting at a bloody photograph now. Honestly, Chrissie, sometimes I wonder about your sanity. I think I'd better refer you to a psychiatrist. Your obsession with Emily is beyond a joke."

Anger rushed in and washed away any fear or commonsense. I advanced towards him. "*My* obsession! What about yours? Why won't you get rid of this fucking photograph and that chair? Why do we have to keep everything the way Emily liked it? Why can't you move on? You're married to *me* now, not her."

I stood inches away from him. And what I saw scared me.

"Sometimes, Chrissie, I wish to God I weren't."

He spun on his heel and left me dumbfounded. The study door slammed behind him and I heard another clatter behind me. I turned, somehow knowing what I would see. The photograph had fallen off the wall again. Only, this time it lay where it couldn't possibly have landed. Six inches from my foot. Without another thought, I stamped on it, smashed the glass and twisted the photograph with both feet until it lay tattered and ruined in a broken frame. I might be losing Joe, but I sure as hell was going to take that bitch Emily with me.

My phone rang. "Private Number" showed on the screen. I answered. A woman laughed in my ear and her words chilled me. "He's mine. He's always been mine and he always will be."

I threw the phone across the room, where it smashed against the wall. I couldn't stay in that room any longer. I raced out of there, sobbing uncontrollably. My mind was all over the place. I couldn't focus or concentrate. I wanted to scream myself hoarse, to tear down every scrap of Emily from this accursed house.

My life was falling apart and I couldn't stop it. I sobbed alone in the kitchen. All I wanted was for Joe to come out of his study, put his arms around me and tell me he believed me. Had he heard the phone ring? Would he believe what I had heard?

But the study door stayed shut.

Maybe half an hour later, fortified with some of the cooking brandy, I knocked on that door. Anger reasserted itself. Why should I knock on a door in my own house? Without waiting for him to reply, I turned the handle and opened the door.

He was staring at his computer screen and took a second or two to realize he wasn't alone. He looked up and his face darkened. "What do you want?" He might have been talking to a complete stranger.

I swallowed, but my mouth was dry. The anger evaporated, leaving only sadness. "I wondered if you were ready to eat yet. I could cook the steaks."

He nodded. "I'll eat mine in here. I have a lot of work to do."

Could he really hurt me any more than he had already? This was Valentine's Day. I had prepared everything for a lovely romantic dinner and now look at us. Two strangers in a wrecked marriage. I hesitated. I had so much to say, but no idea how to say it.

"Was there something else?" His expression gave me no encouragement, so I shook my head and left him alone, closing the door quietly behind me.

In the kitchen, I automatically went through the motions of frying his steak just how he liked it. I cooked mine at the same time, but left it much longer in the pan. I knew I probably wouldn't eat more than a few mouthfuls, if that.

I took particular care with the sauce and sautéed the potatoes to a lovely golden brown. I arranged everything on a plate, ignoring the pâté. I doubted either of us was in the mood for a three-course meal now.

I opened the champagne, poured a glass and added it to the tray, beside his plate and cutlery. Then I carried it into the study.

As I set the tray down in front of him, he pointed at the glass. "Hardly cause for celebration."

"I didn't want it to go to waste," I said, and wondered—as he must have done—why on earth I had opened the bottle in the first place.

He didn't look up at me and I returned to the kitchen and my solitary meal.

I managed four mouthfuls and gave up. My dinner ended up in the waste bin and the washing up went into the barely used dishwasher. I couldn't be bothered to do it myself. Nothing mattered anymore. Not when I was sure I was losing Joe.

I tried to think of ways to convince him of my innocence, but unless he trusted me, nothing would make him believe me. Although why he should think I would want to destroy his lovely gift, I couldn't imagine.

Eventually, at around ten that evening, I pulled myself up and forced myself back into the living room, this time armed with a dustpan and brush in one hand and a bucket, containing stain remover and a soft cloth, in the other.

Everything lay where I had left it. I bent down and picked up the broken glass, bits of shattered frame, petals, and leaves and put them in the bucket, all except the smashed phone which I put in my handbag. I would have to deal with that later. I laid the ripped pieces of the photograph on the nearest occasional table, wincing as I felt a sharp prick. Maybe a tiny shard of glass had stuck itself to the fragment of photograph in my hand. I looked down, opened my hand and saw the droplet of blood oozing out of my thumb. I revealed the shred of photograph—which showed part of the rose stem and that sharp thorn. As I knew it would. For a second, I felt disconnected somehow. Unreal. I sucked my thumb and the bleeding stopped.

I carried on, sweeping up the remaining debris, taking care to make sure I had every fragment of glass. I would vacuum later, of course, but before that, I needed to tackle the red stains on the rug. They looked like bloodstains and the sight of them chilled me.

I scrubbed at the rug until most of the staining was off and just the odd pale pink mark remained, barely noticeable unless you really looked. Hopefully these would fade entirely with time.

I heard the study door open and close but, although Joe must have realized where I was, he didn't come near the living room.

I vacuumed the rug and put my cleaning materials away, threw the contents of the bucket into a strong plastic garbage bag and put it in the bin.

I dreaded the thought of Joe's reaction tomorrow when he realized I had smashed his beloved portrait. The bits of torn photograph were where I had left them, so he would be bound to see them as soon as he walked into the room. I debated whether to remove the evidence, but what was the point? He would know I was the culprit, and this time he would be right. Of course, I shouldn't have done it. All I had done was play right into her hands. Joe would never believe I hadn't destroyed those roses.

My spirits at rock bottom, I climbed the stairs and tiptoed into the bedroom. Joe was already in bed and I could tell from his breathing, he was asleep. No point disturbing him and I couldn't bring myself to climb in with him anyway, so I left him and went into one of the spare rooms. I always kept a bed made up in there, although I hadn't a clue why, as no one ever came to stay. But tonight I was glad of it and, fully clothed, I crept under the duvet, switched off the light, and closed my eyes.

I had never felt so low. How could Joe not believe me? How was I going to make everything right between us? Especially now that I'd smashed that bloody photograph.

———

Somehow, maybe through sheer exhaustion, I must have dozed off for a few minutes because I woke with a start, certain someone was in the room.

"Joe?" I called. No answer. Slowly, I felt the duvet move, as if someone were tugging on it. Steadily, as if with some purpose, it started to move down the bed, as it had on that earlier night. Panic rose inside me. I snapped on the light and watched incredulously as the duvet slid further and further off me.

I screamed. *"Joe!"* But all I heard was a long, low laugh. A female laugh. I grabbed hold of the duvet and started to tug it back up again, but whatever was pulling it was stronger and I was losing the battle.

I screamed and leapt out of bed, shaking from head to foot. I backed away. I could see the mattress moving up and down as if someone were lying on it. Incredibly, I saw an indentation appear on the pillow—the exact shape of a person's head. The duvet moved up the bed again, and, as I watched, unable to move or think straight, the shape appeared to turn on its side, with the duvet pulled up over its shoulders.

I don't know how long I stood there, mesmerized. Did I expect it to turn over and speak to me? I knew no one lay in that bed. But I could make out a shape. *Her* shape—and suddenly I knew. Joe hadn't disposed of that bed. He had merely moved it into a spare room. I had been sleeping in the bed where Emily died and she had thrown me out of it.

"What's the matter with you now?"

I turned to see Joe in the doorway. His sleep hadn't improved his mood or his attitude toward me. But, in a way, I was relieved to see him. Now he would have to believe me.

"Look at the bed!" I said, pointing at it.

"What about it?"

My spirits plummeted again. I knew before I even turned back. The bed was disheveled. Just as I had left it. Emily had gone. Leaving me to explain the inexplicable. Yet again.

"I'm going back to bed," Joe said. "Try not to wake me up again tonight." His voice was like an ice pick, driving into my soul.

He returned to the bedroom and slammed the door.

I sank to the floor, staring at the bed, almost willing its former occupant to reappear. I had a score to settle with her. A few minutes later, I stood, my legs shaky. I wouldn't get any more sleep in that room and couldn't return to our bedroom. I glanced at my watch and saw the time—ten minutes before midnight. This awful Valentine's Day was almost over.

I would go downstairs and make a cup of tea. Maybe that would help steady my nerves. Especially if I added a drop of brandy.

I tiptoed down the landing and was passing our bedroom when I heard a sound. Voices. One male—Joe—and one female.

I threw open the door and saw them.

The bedside lamp cast a warm glow over the room. On the bed, a beautiful couple were making love. She was slender, lithe, and her golden blonde hair reached down to her waist. She was naked, and astride my husband.

She tossed her mane of hair aside, looked over her shoulder at me and smiled.

I breathed her name, "Emily," and she started to laugh. A snicker became a belly laugh. She threw back her head and, as I advanced towards them, Joe came into view. Naked, beneath her, he started to laugh too. I put my hands to my ears to try to block out the sound. I squeezed my eyes shut, hoping that when I opened them again, all I would see was my husband sleeping peacefully, alone. But the laughter told me everything I needed to know.

"Stop it! *Stop it!*" I cried, but they didn't. Their laughter grew louder. I opened my eyes and saw Emily start to ride Joe. He grasped her around her waist, as his hands rose to cup her breasts. And still they laughed, ignoring me as they enjoyed each other.

I couldn't stand it any longer. I had to make them stop.

I looked around and saw the scissors lying on the dressing table. I had no recollection of leaving them there. They were sharp kitchen scissors and had no business being in the bedroom. I grabbed them. Their blades glinted in the lamplight.

Reason deserted me. A force took hold of me and drove me on. I screamed and lunged out with the scissors. I stabbed at Emily. My aim found flesh and drove into it. Once, twice, three times, more. I lost count. My vision blurred, but I kept on stabbing. "*Die*, you bitch. Once and for all. Leave me alone. Leave *us* alone!"

The laughter stopped.

My vision returned.

I dropped the scissors on the floor and stared.

The bed was red with blood. The figure that lay there didn't move.

"Joe?" I whispered. I touched his hair with my right hand and it came away sticky, dripping with his blood. But I had stabbed *Emily*. Where was she? I looked around. She was nowhere to be seen.

I stared down at Joe. Sprawled. Naked. Bloody wounds covered his chest and abdomen. One eye was almost gouged out and, everywhere, blood. So much blood.

I looked down at myself. Blood spattered my dress and I must have had it in my hair too because I could smell it. Horrified, I backed away from that awful scene of carnage and caught sight of myself in the mirror. Hair wild, eyes staring like those of a madwoman, I brushed my face with my hand and left a bloody streak down my right cheek.

From somewhere, I heard a clock chime. Midnight. But we didn't have a chiming clock. That must be Emily's doing. She was mocking me again, now that she had her own way. Now that she had made me release Joe from this world and she could have him all to herself again. For that, surely, was the motive behind all this. If she couldn't have him alive, she would have him dead, before the day of the anniversary of her own death ended. He was with her in some heinous afterlife and I was alone to face the consequences of my dreadful actions.

Something made me go downstairs. We still had landlines. I could have used the one in the bedroom, or even in the hall, but I wanted to get to the study, the only room where I had never felt Emily's presence.

I dialed the emergency services. "I need the police, and an ambulance," I heard myself say in a controlled, detached voice. "There's been a terrible accident."

They arrived a few minutes later and banged on the front door. I stood up from Joe's desk, brushed down my dress and went to let them in. In my hand, I carried a small box. I have it with me still.

Chapter Seven

Of course, they didn't believe me any more than Joe had. I tried to tell them about Emily. About what she had done and what she had driven me to. They decided I wasn't fit to stand trial. Paranoid schizophrenia, they called it, and put me on lithium. And they also locked me up. Put me behind bars and high walls in a maximum security mental hospital, where they left me to rot.

They let me keep my little box though. Every year, on Valentine's Day, I retrieve it from my special hiding place, underneath a floorboard. I'm one of the lucky ones because I have my own room. I only have to mix with the others at mealtimes, and for an hour each evening. I behave myself, you see? I don't get into any trouble, don't make a fuss, and keep my head well below the parapet. There's even been some talk of releasing me. My doctor thinks I'm pretty harmless these days. I've long stopped telling him I always was. They may never have believed me about Emily, but one day, I'm determined they will.

I've been here the longest now. Thirty-five years. I've seen them come and go, from young girls with bewildered stares, through to hardened murderers with a lifetime of cruelty and abuse behind them. All of them with voices in their heads, urging them on.

I never had those. Voices in my head. With the exception of my unlamented father, Emily was my only enemy and I carry a bit of her with me always. In my little box.

I think about Joe often. Wherever he is, I hope he is at peace and will forgive me, but somehow I doubt it. With Emily around to drip poison in his ear, he'll continue to regard me with the contempt I saw in his eyes on that dreadful night, when Emily made me take his life and I lost my own.

Roni stopped writing to me years ago. Her letters had become shorter and shorter and I really don't think she knew what to say to me anymore, so she gave up. Can't say I think about her much, although her dismissal of me hurt like hell at the time.

I haven't had visitors for years. Mostly, I'm happy enough on my own. I've grown accustomed to it.

Today is Valentine's Day, and, as always, I dug out my little box this morning. I turned the key, opened it and the scent of vanilla wafted out at me as always. But something was different this year. Underlying the sweet scent was another, less pleasant aroma. The smell of decay.

I heard a knock at my door. I shut my box as the friendly nurse came in. Niamh. Irish girl, about thirty I think. She used to be a nun, she told me, but left before she took final vows. Didn't have the calling for it, she said. She's a kind person and the only one that doesn't seem to judge me. Today, though, she wasn't alone.

She was grinning broadly. "I have a surprise for you, Chrissie. Look who's come to see you."

I peered at the elderly woman. Her face was familiar. Then I realized.

"Diane? Is it you?"

"Hello, Chrissie."

Still clutching my box, I struggled to my feet. My knees don't work so well these days.

Niamh plumped up the cushions on the two chairs in the room and sat down on one. "There now, sure you'll be wanting to spend some time together, catching up, won't you? Doctor says it's all right, just for ten minutes, as long as I stay with you."

Tears streamed down my face. I don't know why. Diane and I hugged.

"It's been a long time, Chrissie. I didn't know if you'd want to see me."

We parted and I stared at her. Why, after all this time, did *she* want to see *me*? I barely recognized her. Her face was pale, wrinkled and dried out, and although I knew she was around my age, she could easily have been ten years older. She swayed slightly and I steadied her. Clearly she had made a great effort to get here. This wasn't some casual social visit.

"I need to sit down," she said, her breath catching in her throat.

I sat down on my bed and watched Diane lower herself painfully into the other chair. Bad hip by the look of it. Her hair was gray, almost white and her eyes blinked at me from behind thick glasses.

I waited for her to settle comfortably before I asked, "What's brought you here on today of all days, Diane?"

She sighed heavily. Her voice was as fragile as she was. "Barton Grove was empty for years after ... It fell into disrepair. Almost derelict. A couple of years ago, a lovely young couple bought it and spent months and months doing it up. They had a housewarming at the weekend and I went. I wish to God I hadn't."

My heart was pounding. "Why? What happened?"

Diane's hands were trembling and, as she spoke, she gripped the arms of the chair so tightly I could see her knuckles, white and skeletal.

"I smelled it as soon as I stepped in the front door. Vanilla."

Now *my* hands trembled. I clutched the box tighter as Diane spoke.

"I asked Celia about it and she laughed. She said it was a good thing she liked the smell of vanilla, because it seemed to come with the house. Whatever plastering or painting they did, back would come the smell. In *every* room, she said."

Niamh stirred. "Oh to be sure, vanilla's a *lovely* smell. I'm always telling you that, aren't I, Chrissie?" She turned to Diane who stared at her in increasing horror. "Every so often, I come in here and there's this wonderful smell of vanilla. We don't have any in our supplies so I know she must be getting it from somewhere, but will she tell me?" Niamh chuckled, shook her head and turned to me. "You like your little secrets don't you, Chrissie? Like to keep us guessing."

Diane stared straight at me. "I can smell it now."

"So can I," I said. "You know it's the anniversary today."

Diane nodded slowly.

Niamh sniffed. "Oh, yes, there it is again. Lovely." Suddenly her expression changed. "No, there's something different about it this time." She wrinkled her nose. "Oh, no, I don't like that nearly so much."

The box slipped from my fingers, fell onto the carpet and spilled its contents onto the floor, releasing a pungent odor.

Diane hoisted herself out of the chair and backed away, unsteadily, to the door as Niamh sprang up and opened a window.

One by one, I picked up the torn pieces of Emily's photograph and pieced them together as I always did, jigsaw-like, on the clean bedspread. Soon her face stared out at me again. The face of an angel, with the mind of a demon. I found the pieces of her hand, which still clasped her rose. I took my usual care not to prick my finger on the thorn.

That's when I saw it. The rose is different, you see. I'm looking at it now.

No longer perfect, it stinks of putrefaction, its petals brown and withered. A dead rose.

It bothers me. But I don't know why.

About the Author

Following a varied career in sales, advertising and career guidance, Catherine Cavendish is now the full-time author of a number of paranormal, ghostly and Gothic horror novels and novellas.

Her novels include: *The Stones of Landane, Those Who Dwell in Mordenhyrst Hall, The After-Death of Caroline Rand, Nemesis of the Gods* trilogy: *Wrath of the Ancients, Waking the Ancients,* and *Damned by the Ancients, Dark Observation, In Darkness, Shadows Breathe, The Garden of Bewitchment. The Haunting of Henderson Close, The Devil's Serenade, The Pendle Curse* and *Saving Grace Devine.*

The Crow Witch and Other Conjurings is a collection of her previously published and brand new short stories.

Her novellas include: *The Darkest Veil, Linden Manor, Cold Revenge, Miss Abigail's Room, The Demons of Cambian Street, Dark Avenging Angel, The Devil Inside Her,* and *The Second Wife.*

She lives by the sea in Southport, England with her long-suffering husband, and a black cat called Serafina who has never forgotten that her species used to be worshipped in ancient Egypt. She sees no reason why that practice should not continue.

You can connect with Cat here:

Website: catherinecavendish.com/
Facebook: facebook.com/CatherineCavendishWriter
X (formerly Twitter): twitter.com/Cat_Cavendish
Instagram: instagram.com/catcavendish/
Tik Tok: catcavendish
Bluesky @catcavendish.bsky.social

Curious about other Crossroad Press books? Stop by our website:
http://crossroadpress.com
We offer quality writing
in digital, audio, and print formats.

Subscribe to our newsletter on the website homepage and receive a
free eBook.

www.ingramcontent.com/pod-product-compliance
Lightning Source LLC
Chambersburg PA
CBHW022051170626
46808CB00003B/1436